Broken Arrow

Erle Hawke is a drifter who sets out from his distant home in search of his brother. For years he finds no sign of his sibling. Unlike the boiling climate, the search has gone cold. Then, after riding into a sun-bleached town, Hawke is told that there is a ranch out in the arid desert looking for hands. The youngster does not realize that the town locals are lying. They are sending him to his death in the uncharted desert.

As Erle slowly begins to succumb to the ferocious heat, and is running out of precious water, a strange vision appears. As Hawke stares into the shimmering heat-haze, he sees a chilling character riding towards him: an Indian, painted from head to toe, and sat astride a powerful black horse – the mysterious Broken Arrow.

Broken Arrow

Dale Mike Rogers

A Black Horse Western

ROBERT HALE · LONDON

ISBN 978-0-7198-1435-8

Robert Hale Limited
Clerkenwell House
Clerkenwell Green
London EC1R 0HT

www.halebooks.com

Typeset by
Derek Doyle & Associates, Shaw Heath
Printed and bound in Great Britain by
CPI Antony Rowe, Chippenham and Eastbourne

Dedicated to the great actor Matt Smith,
who looks good in a Stetson.

PROLOGUE

If the weathered town had a name it remained unknown to all but those who dwelled within its ill-defined boundaries. There were no markers apart from those that fringed the remote town on the very edge of the featureless prairie. Bleached wooden markers and a handful of crosses leaned into the devastating heat of the deadly land which went on into infinity. Only those most recently erected still had names upon them. The others had faded under the relentless rays of the sun.

The town itself only existed because its original inhabitants had driven wells deep into the underground lakes of water. Dogged determination had located the precious liquid in this otherwise dry landscape.

A small group of townsfolk were still laughing as they stared at the solitary set of hoof tracks that headed through the scattered graves and innocently out into the prairie. His horse's hoofs were the only tracks headed in that direction; anyone who knew this lethal land would have known better than to risk their necks riding into what they all knew as the gateway of Hell.

They had never known anyone to return from that cruel place. It seemed as though the prairie devoured all who ventured into its noisome heat haze.

The townspeople joked and laughed as they recalled the young innocent rider who had believed their lies. To some of their number that memory would prove to be as lethal as the prairie itself.

Earlier that day, shortly before the departure of the drifter five riders had cut through the swirling dust cloud and entered the outskirts of the town. The heavily armed riders had taken rooms in the town's only hotel.

They were waiting for sundown before they would set out on their own perilous journey. Although they intended heading into the same prairie that the young drifter had ridden into, they would be better prepared.

Their leader had gone to his room earlier than the men who followed him. He alone had managed to find a female to share the room with whilst his crew had decided to replenish with hard liquor the fluid they had lost.

The four other men had been in the saloon when the young drifter rode into town and sought information in there. The young man looked as though he had yet to have any call to use a straight razor and was as green as any they had ever encountered.

They watched with amusement when the townsfolk had sent him into the prairie with the false information that he would locate a ranch there where he would find work.

The drifter had been naive enough to swallow every word the locals had dished out to him. The four outlaws sipped their whiskey and watched with amusement as the keen youngster did not even bother to fill his canteens or buy provisions before setting out on his vain quest.

The laughter within the saloon was still as loud as it had been hours earlier. The townsfolk, who had now returned from staring at the young man's tracks, seemed more than happy to have successfully fooled yet another stranger and sent him to his death, like all those who had preceded him.

There was little amusement to be had in the small town, and it seemed as though the local men who graced the settlement's solitary saloon regarded some strangers as fair game. The drinking was accompanied by roars of laughter as they continued to recall their latest victim. Only hardened, well-armed strangers ever escaped their lies. Even in this remote place it seemed that notches on gun grips kept folks honest. All of the local pranksters had steered clear of the four seated men.

As darkness approached and a million stars began to appear in the vast heavens above the remote settlement, the swing doors of the saloon were flung apart and the outlaws' leader marched in. The smile etched into his unshaven features told the four others that his hours with the female had been very satisfying.

But the outlaw leader's smile soon evaporated as the riotous laughter of the ten locals filled his ears. He had no knowledge of what had occurred earlier, and he imagined that the laughter was aimed at him.

The townsfolk in the saloon were still laughing at

the prank they had played upon the drifter as Sheb Dooley approached his men. There was no reason for any of them to know that the man who had just entered the saloon was not just a merciless killer.

Dooley had never had a sense of humour, even at the best of times. Now it seemed to Dooley that they were all laughing at him. His eyes narrowed as a sudden rage swept through his every fibre.

The outlaw leader halted in his tracks halfway across the saloon. His four men had consumed nearly two bottles of whiskey and were in no mood to explain to him what had occurred hours earlier.

Dooley looked around the saloon as the light outside the tinder-dry saloon faded. His eyes darted from one laughing face to another as the citizens of the small settlement continued to rejoice at the memory of the drifter whom they had sent to his death.

While his four henchmen sat impassively and watched, Dooley remained stationary as the barkeep scratched a match along the bar counter and lit the three coal-tar lanterns he had readied. His match touched each of the wicks and light spread through the long bar-room.

Unable to control his fury, Dooley pulled both his

.45s from their holsters and cocked the hammers. He turned to face the men, who were totally unaware of the danger they were in.

'I'll teach you varmints it don't pay to laugh at Sheb Dooley,' he snarled loudly. 'It don't pay at all.'

The eyes of the laughing townsfolk looked at Dooley as he toyed with his guns. They were still laughing when blinding flashes of venomous fury spewed from the barrels of Dooley's weapons. The laughter only stopped when the bullets found each of the jovial men with uncanny accuracy.

Each of the ten local men in the saloon was torn apart by the bullets that ripped through them. Their lifeless forms were sent crashing into the sand-covered floor to start their souls on their journey to meet their Maker. Crimson gore sprayed the otherwise drab saloon in its gory hue as the wooden walls rocked to the deafening echo of gunplay.

In a matter of only a few seconds Dooley had ended the laughter that had filled the saloon. Smoke billowed from his gun barrels and his eyes scanned the twisted bodies scattered upon the floor whilst their blood streamed from the deadly wounds.

'Nobody laughs at Sheb Dooley,' the gunman growled.

The stunned barkeep dropped his match and stared in disbelief at the carnage in front of him. The lantern light made it even more vivid. Every trace of colour drained from his face as Dooley swung around from the bloodshed and approached him.

The barkeep raised his hands.

'I never seen nothing, mister,' he stammered. 'I never seen nothing at all. Don't shoot me.'

'Why would I shoot you?' Dooley asked. 'You weren't laughing.'

The barkeep nodded and swallowed.

'That's right.' He gulped again.

Dooley holstered one of his smoking weapons and began to reload the other. As his four men rose from their chairs and strode to his side Dooley pointed his smoking barrel at the long counter behind the barkeep.

'Whiskey,' he demanded.

The barkeep obliged.

ONE

The shimmering heat haze moved like transparent vipers across the vast prairie as the noonday sun reached the zenith. Every droplet of moisture was sucked from the bleak terrain in strange continuous waves. This was no ordinary land that faced the lone rider as he steered his fatigued mount on towards the distant mesas.

This was a strange place, set somewhere between heaven and hell. The beauty of the landscape belied its true nature. This was a land designed by Satan himself, with a thousand ways to kill the unwary.

The horseman leaned over his saddle horn and stared at his own sweat as it dripped on to the blisteringly hot leather and instantly evaporated.

He glanced at his hands as they teased the long leathers and encouraged the horse ever onwards. His skin was blistered and burned to a hue that almost matched that of his saddle leather.

The denim trousers had been dark blue a month before, but now, as he continued on into the unknown, they were bleached of all colour.

The prairie shimmered all around him as though he were surrounded by mocking phantoms. There was no escape for the weary horseman. Wherever he cast his attention the hot burning air continued to taunt his senses.

Erle Hawke gripped his reins tightly and tried to remember how and why he had ridden so willingly into this devilish place. He reached down to his canteen and was about to lift it from his saddle horn when he realized that it was empty. There was not one droplet of the precious liquid remaining. Then his eyes stared down at the sweat-drenched horse.

Hawke had given the last of his water to the animal just after sunrise, he recalled. He rubbed his throat and selfishly regretted that gallant decision.

He was being slowly cooked, as though he were little more than a pig on a spit. The heat blazed down from the cloudless sky and reflected off the white sand. He was merely a lump of meat caught in the middle.

His red-raw eyes were too sore to blink without pain and yet he blinked. Salt was caked in the corners of each burning eye, tormenting him, but he knew that the worst was yet to come. Death would follow soon enough when there was no more torture left to inflict upon him.

Hawke gazed around the desolate scene. Nothing was as it seemed in the pitiless terrain that surrounded the rider. A thousand phantoms mocked the young horseman wherever he looked. The air itself was alive. Soon it would be the only thing alive, Hawke reckoned.

He thought about the journey he had undertaken. Every passing day had been hotter than the last; the visions had become more mysterious.

Hawke found himself in a place that was beyond understanding. Sweat had soaked his clothing, then, as the sun grew more powerful, it had dried again. Day after day he had suffered the same ritual. Until now he had had water but now that was little more than a memory.

Every fibre of his being told Hawke that this would be the final day. There was no way of surviving in this oven without water.

He pressed the dying mount to keep walking on. Like Hawke it was headed towards its own demise. The young rider looked all around him. The heat haze seemed to be getting denser.

It burned at his face. Even his Stetson was unable to protect his skin against the relentless rays of the sun.

There was no hiding place.

Hawke had found himself drawn into a land which did not forgive anyone who dared venture across its boundaries. It was too late for him, he wearily thought.

Far too late.

He had made a mistake days earlier and now he was paying for that error of judgement. He had ridden into the very bowels of Hell and now they were squeezing the life out of him.

Hawke tried to suck in air but only dust filled his dry mouth. He coughed, then felt himself dismounting. There was no intention in it. He just slid from his saddle and landed in the dry ground, beside the hoofs of his mount.

He lay there for few moments, unable to do anything except stare into the mist, which rose all around his aching body. Eventually he rolled on to his belly and forced his weary form up on to his elbows.

So many questions filled his dulled senses. Why was he here? For what reason had he ridden to this place? His memory was starved of answers just as his body was starving from lack of water.

He lifted his head and tried to see through the haze.

The horse stood beside him. There was little salvation in its lean shadow. Then he reached up to the stirrup and hauled himself up on to his knees.

Hawke rested and held on to the stirrup as the heat of the hot earth burned through his pants' knees. He tried to swallow but there was no spittle in his dry mouth.

Then he saw something.

There was no sound but his screwed-up eyes saw a dark image moving beyond the suffocating heat haze. Hawke tried to stand but his legs refused to obey the simple command. All he could do was stare at the fragmented image as it gradually moved towards him and grew larger.

Hawke released his grip on the stirrup and dropped his hand to his holster. He slid the palm of his gloved hand over the .45 and drew it.

Before he had time to aim the weapon he heard a sound.

An arrow cut through the heat haze and hit the barrel of the Colt. The weapon was torn from his grip. Hawke stared in awe at the gun on the sand and the arrow beside it.

Hawke was about to retrieve his gun when he heard hoofs nearing him. He lifted his head and watched helplessly as the shimmering vision began to take form.

Within seconds he was looking up at a horse and rider. The blinding rays of the merciless sun masked what he was peering upon. Hawke lifted his arm and used his hand to shield his eyes. His jaw dropped.

Terror filled the youngster.

TWO

Erle Hawke had been scared many times before but never had he been filled with terror. The fearsome sight was more than his dazed mind had envisaged. He rocked on the burning earth and tried to understand what he was looking upon. The awesome figure resembled something created in the nightmares of a madman. His tongue traced his cracked lips whilst his mind raced. All he could do was stare up at the rider with the bow in his hands and wonder when the deadly arrow would be released. The point of the arrow was needle sharp. It glinted in the rays of the sun.

Hawke tilted his head back. He focused along the

shaft of the deadly projectile to the torso of the rider. The sun dazzled his sore eyes, yet he refused to turn away.

Some things were best faced full on. There were some things that even a half-dead horseman could not escape by closing his sore eyes.

The rider was silent. As silent as death.

Hawke reached to the stirrup of his mount and grabbed it again. Mustering every scrap of his dwindling strength he pulled himself up off the hot ground until he felt the grit beneath his boot leather again.

He rested against the saddle and squinted.

He could see more clearly now, and still he did not believe what he was looking upon. Nothing had prepared Hawke for the sight that faced him. Hawke's eyes widened.

Since childhood he had heard tales of Indians but in all his days as a drifter he had never actually encountered any. Not until now.

This Indian was nothing like any in the stories he had been raised upon. Even the worst of those tales had never described anything like the strange creature he faced. Hawke lowered his gaze upon the mount but even the beast seemed monstrous to his naive mind.

The creature was black. All of its trimmings were of a similar hue. He looked back up at the bowman.

The only thing that told Hawke he was looking at an Indian at all was the fact that upon the lowered head of the archer was perched a strange feathered headdress. The headdress seemed different from the crude dime novel illustrations he had been raised on. This was not a white-eagle-feathered war bonnet but something far more macabre. It looked as though a black-winged crow had been ripped apart and mounted.

This was no attractive headdress but an omen of something far darker. A horror that clawed at the very soul of anyone who cast their eyes upon it.

Hawke rubbed his painful eyes. Yet they did not lie to him. They revealed the truth. The whole frightening truth.

Every part of the rider was covered in black pigment.

Not one scrap of his natural skin was visible to Hawke.

The face was as black as a raven's wing. Upon the black a series of white lines had been painted in such a way as to completely obliterate any recognizable features. The application of the pigment distorted the features to such an extent that they were totally unlike any other face Hawke had ever seen.

Only the eyes told Hawke that he was actually looking at another man. They glared down at him with unblinking coldness and intensity. They gave no hint of what was yet to come; not one clue as to why this strange creature had emerged from the baleful heat haze at all.

'Who are you?' Hawke vainly cried out.

There was no answer. A horrifying thought raced through Hawke's young mind. Was this creature going to kill him because he had unwarily defiled some religious sanctuary and this dark bowman been spirited here simply to send an arrow through his heart? Was that it?

Hawke studied the rest of the rider.

He was half naked, as though in defiance of the rays of the relentless sun. Below his black-painted torso he wore fringed black trousers. Hawke had never seen an image of an Indian that looked anything remotely like this strange apparition.

Every sinew of the young drifter's being ached as he somehow retained his balance against his horse but, with a defiance that only youth could summon up, Hawke shook his fist at the silent horseman.

'Why don't you fire that arrow?' he raged. 'I'm not scared of you. Kill me.'

The dark horseman remained unmoved and as silent as the grave. He kept the arrow in his bow aimed down at the defenceless Hawke.

A mocking breeze cut across the vast plain. Loose grit blew across both Indian and drifter, and yet neither seemed to notice or care. Again Hawke shouted his defiance.

'Shoot that damn arrow if you've a mind. That's what you intend doing, ain't it?'

The rider remained as still as a statue. His bow was still arched as though ready to release its arrow at any moment.

'Shoot.' Hawke croaked. 'I don't give a damn. I'm already dead but at least I'm smart enough to know it. Erle Hawke ain't feared of no one.'

The rider tilted his head, then relaxed the taut bowstring and lowered it. His curled finger gripped the arrow as he pulled the large water bag free from across his horse's shoulders.

As the bewildered Hawke stood watching in amazement the Indian lowered the bag to the ground and pulled back on his crude rope reins.

The black stallion took two steps backwards, then stopped.

Hawke stared at the damp water bag.

His eyes then looked at the horseman.

The expressionless face stared at Hawke, then the Indian raised a finger and pointed at the bag. He made no sound.

Hawke staggered forward and fell to his knees beside the bag. He pulled the wooden stopper, lifted the neck of the bag to his lips and drank.

If life tasted of anything it tasted of water. Hawke was breathing heavily as he lowered the water bag from his lips. He looked up, then saw the horseman turn his mount and ride into the shimmering heat haze.

As he rested on his knees his mount stepped next to him. Hawke removed his hat, placed it on the sand and filled it with the precious liquid.

As Hawke's stallion began to drink, he saw something fall from the mysterious horseman's hand on to the sand. He stared ahead and saw the broken arrow on the ground a few feet from where he stood. He staggered forward and snatched both segments of the arrow up and looked at it. Hawke thought for a moment and started to nod to himself.

'Broken Arrow,' he whispered. 'So that's your name.'

THREE

Darkness had been a welcome relief from the relentless sun which had tortured Erle Hawke for hours. He felt the frost on his face and was thankful for its merciful soothing. Hawke tossed more kindling into the centre of his campfire and then stared at the fiery inferno he had created. The flames of the campfire seemed to touch the stars far above the youngster. A million red sparks danced upward from the fire and floated all around him.

Hawke felt relieved that he had survived until nightfall in this unholy prairie. Yet there was no self-satisfied gloating in the young drifter, for he knew that he owed his life to the strange figure who, he believed, was called Broken Arrow.

Hawke sat with his back against his saddle and stared at the water bag beside him. The difference between life and death lay inside that large leather bag. He lay down, rested his head against the saddle and stared at the flickering flames of his campfire. He then pulled his blanket over his shoulders and tried to get some sleep. The trouble was that it was not that easy. Every time he closed his eyes he saw the image of the man who had mysteriously saved him from dying of thirst hours before.

The haunting memory of the man covered in black pigment refused to be forgotten. The image of the black face covered in white lines troubled Hawke.

Who was Broken Arrow? Why had he suddenly lowered his lethal bow and given him a bag filled with water?

The thought burned into the very soul of the young man like a torturous branding-iron. He tried to sleep but it proved impossible. No man with even a hint of curiosity in him could simply cast such images aside and sleep. They had been carved into his mind and would remain there for eternity.

Hawke gazed into the hypnotic flames but found no place for his restless brain to rest. They simply stimulated more unanswerable questions.

He threw the blanket off his aching body and sat upright for the umpteenth time.

Who was the man hidden under layers of pigment? Why had he appeared and then disappeared? It made no sense to the drifter, no matter how many times he considered it. Why had he hidden his features?

Was he an Indian? If so, why would an Indian have helped him by giving him water?

So many questions.

All unanswered.

Hawke peered through the dancing firelight at his tethered mount. It had drunk more water than he had and almost looked its old self. The stallion's head was no longer lowered as if waiting for the Grim Reaper. Now the horse seemed alert as it silently looked all around the vast prairie that surrounded them.

Just like its master the animal seemed unable to relax. Hawke watched as the handsome horse looked in all directions as if it feared attack.

Was the stallion just nervous, or had its keen instincts detected danger out beyond the range of the campfire's light?

His young mind desired answers and yet there were none.

Hawke rose, stood in his stockinged feet beside the fire and scanned the darkness. He could feel the warmth of the flames as they licked the dry air. Hawke stooped, picked up more of the kindling he had gathered earlier and tossed it on to the fire.

More crimson sparks erupted and floated towards the stars as the fire's hunger was fed.

Hawke was about to sit down again next to his saddle when he heard something far out in the dark terrain. He stepped towards the saddle and looked out into the blackness. His heart was racing.

Yet no matter how hard his narrowed eyes strained to see they could not detect what his ears had heard.

Nervously Hawke rubbed his face. He had imagined it, he told himself. He was tired and needed rest.

His mind darted back to the vision of Broken Arrow. He shook as though a chill had traced his backbone, but there had been no chill.

Only a memory.

Hawke sat down and dragged his saddle-bags towards him. He searched for and then found a tobacco pouch. His fingers fumbled and found a thin paper. He gently sprinkled the tobacco shreds on to the paper. A few rolls, then he raised the gummed edge to his tongue.

He poked the cigarette between his lips and crawled towards the fire. He lifted a burning twig, and touched the tip of the cigarette and inhaled its smoke.

Hawke savoured the aroma of the tobacco, then returned the pouch to his saddle-bag. His eyes darted around in search of what or who might have made the noise, which had alerted him that he was not alone in this devilish place. It had not been his imagination, he thought. He was too tired to imagine anything.

A coyote howled off in the far distance. Hawke inhaled more smoke and stared through it as it filtered through his lips.

The scarlet light of his campfire danced on clumps of sagebrush and twisted cactus which surrounded his resting place. The more he strained to see the more his tired eyes played tricks on him.

He silently cursed the darkness. It was as unrevealing as the damned heat haze had been. Both seemed to mock the young cowboy.

Through the cigarette smoke Hawke recalled how he had come to ride into this place. He realized, too late now, that he had taken the word of liars as being truthful. As always, he had believed the townsfolk who had assured him that he would find work on a ranch about fifty miles from their small settlement. For honest men like Hawke believe that all other men are as honest as he. He would never send anyone into a potentially deadly prairie; innocently he believed that no one else would.

His naive trust in the honesty of others had proved to be his downfall. Regretfully, he had learned that not everyone was the same as he was himself.

Hawke had ridden willingly into the increasingly dangerous prairie after accepting the townsfolk's word as gospel. Far too late had he realized that the they had lied to him and sent him to his doom.

It was a mistake that still might prove deadly.

The young drifter sucked in the last of the smoke from the crudely rolled cigarette and flicked it into the flames. He was picking tobacco from his tongue when he heard another sound.

He swung on his knees and dragged his gun from

its holster. The sound was not the same as the one he had heard previously, he thought.

It was different.

Hawke rose to his full height and walked round the fire with his gun held at hip level. His finger stroked the trigger of his weapon as his eyes searched the darkness. Then he remembered the ominous figure of Broken Arrow.

What if it were the mysterious Broken Arrow moving out there in the dark? He dared not fire unless he was certain of his target. The last thing the young drifter wanted to do was shoot at the very man who had saved him from dying painfully of thirst.

He stood and gazed into the blackness. He had to be certain. Hawke lowered his .45. He was about to return to his bedroll when to his surprise he saw the light of torches far off in the distance. Horsemen were riding in single file.

Hawke counted them.

There were four raised torches, about ten miles from his campsite. He edged away from the fire and squinted out into the distance. Four torches meant at least that number of riders, he concluded. Who in their right minds would venture into this uncharted land?

That was an even more taunting question than the one which had been gnawing at his innards concerning the eerie Broken Arrow. Who would willingly ride into this devilish terrain? He strained to focus but it was impossible. The only things he could see clearly were the raised torches.

Hawke knew that they were riding further away from his campsite. That was at least something for the young drifter to feel confident about.

He pushed his Colt into its holster and watched as the lights grew ever dimmer. For some reason they were travelling away from him, he reasoned. They were not headed towards the distant settlement far behind him. They were headed deeper into this unholy land.

Why would anyone do that?

If there were any more towns in that direction there would be signs. There would be railroad tracks, or at least stagecoach trails. As far as Hawke could tell there was nothing in the direction the horsemen were riding.

Hawke slowly shook his head. He pondered the conundrum until the torchlights faded from sight. He knew that men do not head across a deadly prairie unless they are going somewhere.

Unlike himself, they were not lost.

'Who in tarnation are they?' Hawke muttered curiously. 'And where are they headed?'

FOUR

There was a solemn silence in the streets of the town. It gnawed at the hearts of the men, women and children as they slowly laboured to carry the ten bodies from the saloon to the dusty outskirts of the remote settlement. The sounds of unseen animals echoed around the weathered buildings as slowly a few of the more muscular of their number started to dig holes in the dry ground sand.

Not a word had been spoken by any of them as one by one they laid the bodies of their dead to rest. For more than two hours they had worked by lantern light as black storm clouds gathered across the brooding sky.

At last, as the earth was shovelled on to the last of

the unmarked graves an eerie sound attracted their attention. The women hustled their children and raced back into town towards their homes. Their brawny menfolk remained at the burial ground and tried to figure out where the noise was coming from.

'What is that?' one of the men asked, resting his shovel on his shoulder.

'Horses,' Another responded.

'He's right,' a third fearfully agreed. 'It is horses.'

The dozen or so men moved slowly from the graveyard down towards the town, but their pace increased as the sound of approaching hoofs grew louder. As the men hurried towards the deserted streets they shied away from every shadow. Their eyes darted to each and every dark corner. Baying coyotes in the distance mocked the scared men and howled loudly enough to rival the pounding hoof-beats. The men were falling over one another as they made their way to where the first of the town's buildings stood.

A fearful dread filled their souls.

What if it was the deadly five outlaws returning to add more notches to their gun grips? What if they had not yet quenched their thirst for blood? The thoughts were as chilling as the night air, but they remained unsaid as the men ventured towards the pools of light cast by their few street lanterns.

The dirt-begrimed men scrambled across the last few yards of the wide trail towards the building and pressed their backs against its wall. The porch gave them good cover and they remained pressed up to the wall to await the return of the five outlaws.

They huddled together on the boardwalk as their hysterical wives called out for the menfolk to return to them. The men knew that to move away from the cover might prove to be a fatal mistake. For long moments none of them said a word as the sound grew ever louder.

'I hear riders,' a gruff figure said at last.

The others nodded in agreement.

The sound of pounding horses' hoofs came louder and louder. It was like the warnings of Apache war drums. None of the townsfolk were armed as they had wrongly thought that nobody would ride into their remote settlement while they were burying their dead. Now they had time to regret their error of judgement.

They wanted to flee.

Yet none of them seemed to be able to command

obedience from their lower limbs. They simply stood beneath the porch overhang and waited until their eyes could tell them who was approaching their town.

Like cornered jack rabbits caught in the sights of a scattergun they squinted long and hard. From the darkest parts of the trail they suddenly saw the dust-caked riders emerge over a rise. A flock of prairie hens scattered from their hiding-places amid the sagebrush as the horses cut a trail down the sandy slope towards the unusually quiet town and its frugal illumination. The three horsemen steered their horses on to the dusty road and continued into the heart of the small settlement towards the light that was glimmering out from the saloon.

They looked more like phantoms than living riders. There were three of them and they were trotting towards the onlookers at a slow, deliberate pace. Only their tin stars seemed to have escaped the dust that covered both riders and horses.

'Who is that?' one of the townsfolk asked fearfully.

'That's the territorial marshal,' another answered.

'And his deputies,' added a third.

The dozen pairs of eyes focused on the dust-caked horsemen as they cantered into the main street and drew rein outside the saloon. The towns-folk leapt down from their hiding-place beneath the porch and raced towards the three riders.

The startled lawmen steadied their mounts and watched as the excitable townsfolk ran towards them.

Marshal Bob Styles rubbed the dust from his features and stared at the running men. He was confused, and his gloved fingers stroked his long moustache. He glanced to his deputies, Ned Hackman and Jody Tyler, and raised his eyebrows.

'It looks like they're glad to see us, boys,' he muttered.

The townsmen stopped in front of the three horses. They looked up at the lawmen the way some men look at their idols.

'What's going on here?' Styles asked, brushing the dust from his clothing.

'You gotta help us, Marshal.'

Styles paused and looked down at the faces of the men. He had seen many expressions over the years but never before had he seen grown men look so utterly terrified. He leaned forward and spoke to the closest of the men.

'What you boys carrying them shovels for?' the lawman asked, curiously.

'We've been burying our dead, Marshal.'

The answer stunned the lawmen. Styles straightened up on his saddle and turned his head towards his deputies. He looped his leg over his cantle and dismounted. The tall marshal moved towards the crowd.

'You've been burying your dead?' he repeated.

It seemed as though every man in the crowd nodded at exactly the same moment.

'Yep. Twelve of them, Marshal,' one of the men said, pointing to the disturbed sand. 'We just buried twelve of our boys over yonder.'

Styles indicated for his deputies to dismount. He rested his knuckles on his gun grips and stepped up on to the boardwalk outside the saloon. No sooner had the marshal reached up and placed his gloved hand on the top of the swing doors than his eyes saw the evidence of the carnage within. The three lanterns were still on the long bar counter, casting their light across the floorboards. Their light left nothing to the lawman's imagination.

Styles entered the saloon and swallowed hard.

There was so much blood spread across the floor that it looked as though someone had slaughtered a steer in the centre of the saloon. The marshal tilted his head at his deputies and issued instructions.

'Water and grain our horses, boys,' he whispered angrily. 'We got us some really bad *hombres* to rope.'

Sheb Dooley led his four followers around the very edge of the prairie where moonlit mountains rose over the empty land. Dooley was the only one of his gang who did not hold a flaming torch to guide his way. He did not require the help of torchlight. The hardened outlaw knew the prairie like the back of his hand for he had travelled this way many times since his chance discovery of the town a year earlier.

His discovery would change everything for the five outlaws in a way none of them, including Dooley, had yet to realize.

As the five horsemen entered a narrow canyon Dooley raised his arm and stopped his followers. Dust drifted up into the moonlight. With the air of a Mongol warlord the outlaw leader dismounted and held his long leathers in his hand as he turned back and stared out across the vast prairie.

Dooley was confident in his unopposed leadership of the men around him, for he held a secret in the dark recesses of his mind that none of the others possessed.

He alone knew the way to and from their ultimate destination. Without him none of the outlaws who flanked him would ever escape this place.

Eb Reece reined in and dropped his torch. Like a spear the flaming rod embedded itself into the soft earth as he too dismounted. Reece moved to the side of Dooley.

'What you looking at, Sheb?' Reece asked.

Dooley remained motionless. His eyes stared out into the moonlit prairie at the small pinpoint of light far in the distance.

'I'm looking at that campfire, Eb,' Dooley replied. His gloved hands pulled a cigar from his pocket; he raised it to his mouth and bit off its tip. He spat the small fragment of tobacco to the ground and struck a match across his belt buckle. He cupped its flame and raised it to his cigar, then drew, filling his lungs with smoke.

Joe Landon, Lee Chandler and Poke Janson stopped their horses beside the other mounts.

Reece pushed the brim of his Stetson off his brow

43

and looked to where Dooley was concentrating. His narrowed eyes could barely see the campfire.

'That's gotta be the young drifter.' He chuckled.

Dooley inhaled the smoke of his cigar deep into his lungs and glanced across at Reece.

'Who?' he asked. 'What damn drifter?'

Landon dismounted and led his horse to where the two men were standing.

'You was having some shuteye, Sheb,' Landon informed his leader. 'You didn't get to see the wet-nosed drifter when he showed up back at Diablo.'

Dooley turned his head to stare at Landon. 'What's so funny?'

Chandler rammed his torch into the ground and moved to join Dooley, Reece and Landon. He laughed.

'It was real funny,' Chandler chortled. 'We was in the saloon when this young drifter came in and asked if there was any ranch work, Sheb.'

'The critters in Diablo told him there was,' Janson added, easing his aching bones off the shoulders of his horse. 'They sent him into the prairie. They said there was a ranch out here.'

'The dumb drifter swallowed their tall tale hook, line and sinker.' Reece smiled. 'He jumped back on his horse and rode out.'

Dooley was beginning to understand why his men were so amused by the naive youngster.

'So he just took their word for it, huh?'

Reece nodded. 'That kid must be close to death by now. He never even had the brains to get himself provisions or extra water, Sheb.'

Landon turned back to their mounts. 'He's probably still looking for that damn ranch. He ain't never gonna find it though. Not out here.'

Dooley savoured the smoke of his cigar.

'As long as he don't get in our way I reckon he ain't worth troubling ourselves about,' he said.

'Don't go fretting.' Reece pulled his hat brim down. 'He ain't no threat to us, Sheb. He's just a kid.'

Dooley gave a nod, gripped the cigar between his teeth and puffed enthusiastically. 'So he's just a snot-nosed drifter who is dumb enough to be looking for a ranch that ain't even there?'

'Yep.' Reece laughed.

Dooley smiled cruelly. 'Ain't that just a crying shame, boys?'

The outlaws laughed.

Chandler pulled one of his canteens from his

saddle horn and unscrewed its stopper. 'I figure he must be dead by now or as damn close to it as a varmint can get without water and grub. That dumb critter rode into the prairie with less than a canteen of water.'

Dooley grinned. 'Good.'

'Suicidal.' Reece laughed. 'Just plain suicidal.'

'Leastways he won't be bothering us none.' Smoke filtered through Dooley's teeth.

'Nobody can survive out there in the prairie without water, Sheb.' Janson smiled. 'Not for long anyway.'

Dooley spun on his heels to face his men.

'Damn right, Poke,' Dooley agreed. 'C'mon. We still got us a long ride before we get to where we're headed. That drifter will be dead soon enough.'

FIVE

Deep within the narrow confines of the deadly canyon the blinding dust swirled unchecked as it had done since time itself had begun. Centuries had come and gone yet the cruel canyon still had an appetite for fresh meat. The bleached bones of men and beasts alike lay scattered along its length like hideous markers. Not even the moonlight could lessen their stark warning to those who managed to cross the prairie and reach this ominous place.

It was as though the prairie were guarding this secluded and forgotten place. It protected it from those who might learn its secrets.

Few men had ever reached the canyon. Even fewer had discovered the truth of this cheerless outpost. Only one had managed to escape its clutches and venture back to the land of the living before retracing his tracks and returning.

Dooley was that man.

Some said that only a fool or a madman would even attempt to set foot on the prairie, let alone continue on to the notorious canyon. The murderous incident in the saloon had proved that Dooley was indeed a madman and nursed a merciless rage against anyone he thought was making him look like a fool. Yet, like many outlaw leaders, Dooley had not only killed innocent people with his unholy gun skills, he had also put fear in to the very guts of the men he had chosen to ride with him.

Fear was the one thing all ruthless killers relied upon to keep their followers in check. Dooley had ensured that Reece, Landon, Chandler and Janson would never question him again. He had shown them what happened when anyone riled him.

Yet, apart from all his other qualities, the infamous outlaw leader was a skilled tracker; there were few men who could equal his ability to ride through hostile landscapes and return unscathed. He was also cursed by avarice.

Most sane men would never have even considered travelling back into a terrain which had nearly claimed their lives. But Dooley was not sane, neither was he burdened with doubt. He was in thrall to the alluring promise of untold treasure at the end of their quest.

Like all mirages of treasure-trove, it had snared Dooley with its barbarous hook. He was being reeled in by the thought of what might be waiting for him at the end of his quest. Even sane men found that devilish attraction hard to resist. The West was littered with the bleached bones of men who had hunted gold.

Like so many others he had an insatiable appetite for wealth. Greed had always ruled Dooley. It showed no signs of abating.

The bells of San Angelo had not rung out for more than a hundred years. The isolated mission had remained abandoned since the last of its monks had perished. No living soul knew how the monks had met their fate but the inhospitable climate had more than its share of blame.

Few living creatures ever survived long in the depths of the canyon. The windswept land and blazing sun were designed for creatures created by the Devil and not those who followed a gentler deity.

The monks who had originally built the mission had brought many things with them, including abundant supplies, and when they had come across a spring of crystal-clear water everything seemed to be fine. Soon, however, they learned that an abundant supply of even the sweetest water cannot tame a land that refuses to be tamed.

None of their crops grew.

The very soil appeared to be poisoned or cursed.

The monks realized far too late that they had entered a place where no amount of prayers could be blessed. This was the domain of Satan.

The canyon was like the prairie that surrounded the mission's adobe walls. It was perilous. There seemed to be no crop that would grow in its sandy soil. Soon the inevitable happened and one by one the monks perished.

Then the two mighty bells in the mission's lofty tower ceased ringing out and fell silent. The mission had proved to be nothing more than a vain folly.

Over the decades that followed the once solid

structure crumbled as the relentless wind and crippling heat took their toll.

The prairie took no prisoners. It was merciless in its destruction.

Yet San Angelo had a secret which some said had died with the last of its intrepid monks. Somewhere within its decaying walls there was a fortune in Spanish gold. Ingots and ornaments cast from the finest gold lay buried somewhere within the boundaries of the mission. Spanish gold coins and precious jewels of incalculable value also shared their hiding-place.

Men had not buried the treasure. It had been buried by a remorseless and hostile climate. A century of windswept grit sent by the Devil himself had achieved something no mere man could have done.

To most who had heard the stories of the lost treasure it seemed to be nothing more than a tall tale. A hundred years had only made the stories seem ludicrous, but not to Dooley. He knew the truth.

Sheb Dooley was the only living person to know where the mission was, but even he did not know where its treasure was hidden. Stumbling upon a few golden Spanish coins, Dooley had become aware that all the vague stories were true.

He had seen with his own eyes that it had not been the monks who had secreted their fortune.

The prairie had done that. Although a century of drifting dust had buried most of the Spanish gold from view it had failed to hide it all. The ruthless outlaw had a few of the hoard's countless trinkets in his pocket. Even half-dead, as he had been the last time he had ridden this trail, Dooley had been smart enough to realize that there was more.

All he had to do was find it.

That was why the outlaw had brought four others with him into the land known for its propensity to destroy anything that dared venture across it.

Dooley felt in his guts that no one man could find and carry off such a treasure trove alone. He needed help if he were to salvage all of the priceless treasure.

The five riders rode deeper and deeper into the shadows of the narrow canyon. Even in the dead of night the high walls of the canyon gave off the accumulated heat that they had absorbed during the day.

Sweat trailed down their faces as they urged their

mounts ever onward. With each stride of their horses' legs the heat grew.

Greed had the ability to lure men into the most dangerous of places. It made them willing to risk their very necks in order to set their eyes and hands upon the gleaming gold that Dooley had promised them they would soon find.

They rode on.

SIX

Sleep was no longer an option for the young drifter. Not since he had seen the fiery torches of the distant riders as they proceeded towards the canyon had he slept. Curiosity was the only mistress young Erle Hawke had ever had. It had torn him away from his home in pursuit of his elder brother. As with so many youngsters the thought of adventure and the hope that one day he might find his long lost sibling had spurred the youthful drifter ever deeper into the wilds of the West.

Hawke had tried to sleep after he had seen the riders' torches off in the distance but curiosity had not allowed him to forget. He had to wonder. Like all mistresses the question simply would not stop nagging at his mind until he defied his tiredness and resolved to discover who the riders were and where they had gone.

Trailing the horsemen was not the smartest thing for anyone to do. Hawke had no idea who the torch-toting riders were, and he wanted to find out.

The outlaws who had looked back at his campfire had been correct. He was totally naive and still wet behind the ears.

It had not even occurred to Hawke that he might be riding into trouble. For the last day or so it seemed as though he had been courting death anyway.

He lifted his fender and hooked it on to the saddle horn. As he secured his cinch strap his eyes focused through the campfire smoke at the distant mountain range. It was still dark but the thought of discovering where the riders were headed filled Hawke's mind.

A distant lightning flash alerted both man and horse to the distant storm: a storm that was heading their way. Clouds were doing battle as they approached. A fork of lightning crackled and descended earthward. Hawke patted his stallion's neck and resumed saddling the nervous animal.

Hawke tightened the leathers and looped them under the canvas cinch strap. He dropped the fender, then turned round, lifted the large water bag off the sand and carefully hung it from the saddle horn.

Without even realizing it his eyes vainly searched for Broken Arrow out in the tinder-dry brush that surrounded his makeshift camp.

Hawke grabbed the saddle horn, stepped into his stirrup and hoisted himself up on to shoulders of the tall horse. He carefully teased his reins and swung the horse around until it faced the place where he had last seen the torchlight.

His mind raced.

Who were the riders?

He tapped his spurs and started the horse moving. Hawke wondered where the men were headed. He hoped it was to a place where there was plenty of water and shade. Maybe they knew of a town out there, he thought.

Maybe they knew where there was an Eden in this Hell.

Hawke tapped his spurs again.

As the stallion gathered pace Hawke had another thought. It caused him to stand in his stirrups so that he could survey the bleak terrain that surrounded him. A land dotted with strange Joshua trees and cactus. A land scattered with sagebrush and the bones of those who had ridden this way before him.

His eyes narrowed as they searched for his strange benefactor.

Where, he wondered, was Broken Arrow?

Although Hawke had not seen the Indian since he had vanished back into the oppressive heat haze, something kept nagging at the drifter. Hawke felt that every move he made was being observed by the man daubed in black pigment.

Who was Broken Arrow?

A bead of sweat defied the cooling air and trailed down his face from his hat brim. It followed the shape of his jaw and dripped on to his bandanna. Hawke suddenly felt fear tear through him like a jagged knife. Such a fear as only a man with no answers to his many questions could feel.

Again he spurred, this time with more urgency. Hawke aimed the head of his intrepid stallion at the distant mountains.

The horse increased its speed.

Hawke whipped his long leathers across the

flanks of his thundering horse. With each long stride of his stallion the youngster kept looking all around him. A mighty eruption of thunder shook the air as the storm came closer but Hawke barely noticed. All he could think about was the rider of the black horse. He had no fear of what he was riding blindly towards, except of the one man who might be hiding somewhere out there.

Even though Broken Arrow had saved his life only hours earlier by giving him the water bag, Hawke still feared him more than he feared the unknown riders he was chasing.

There had been something unnerving about the mysterious Broken Arrow. His appearance was unlike any other man he had ever set eyes upon. Just thinking about him made Hawke shake with fear as he urged his mount on.

He whipped the tails of his reins again.

The fact that Broken Arrow had been daubed in black pigment was probably why Hawke could not get the image out of his mind. He had never imagined in his wildest dreams that he would ever meet anyone so well disguised as the Indian.

If in fact he was an Indian.

Hawke strained to see what lay ahead as he thrust

his spurs into the flanks of his stallion. The walls of the canyon grew higher as he drew closer to them.

The moonlight highlighted their jagged outline.

Hawke had never seen anything like the sight which now faced him. He refused to stop or turn back.

Hawke forged on into the unknown.

By his reckoning there was no choice. It was too far to try to return back to the town far behind him, he thought. He had to continue.

He could not remain in the prairie.

That would mean just waiting to die.

The drifter had no intention of dying, yet chasing the riders who had held their torches high as they headed into the canyon was dangerous, he imagined. He had no idea what they would do once they set eyes upon him.

Hawke looked to both sides again.

Some strange feeling gripped at his very heart. Again he felt that he was being observed.

Another bead of sweat rolled down his face.

Somewhere out there in the darkness Broken Arrow was watching his every move: Hawke was certain of it. He urged the stallion to increase its pace again, yet he felt no safer.

Instinctively he knew that he should not be afraid of a man who had already saved his life, but he could not help himself. Terror gripped at his very innards. Hawke was terrified of encountering Broken Arrow again.

The storm erupted again far above him. He glanced up and saw the gathering clouds. To the drifter they seemed alive as they rippled with deadly white flashes.

A splinter of the storm's fury carved a route down from the crashing clouds directly in front of the charging stallion.

A tall three-armed cactus was hit and exploded as though someone had thrown dynamite at it. The horse shied, but Hawke managed to maintain control as he steered around the smouldering debris.

Fear filled his soul but he gritted his teeth and forged on the distant mountain range.

Yet the faster his stallion galloped the more Hawke's mind reasoned that no matter how fast he travelled he could never outride his own fear.

Fear had a habit of keeping pace.

SEVEN

Marshal Bob Styles led his deputies through the darkness deeper and deeper into the vast prairie. The town without a name was far behind them now and getting further away with each jab of their rusted spurs. Styles knew that he and his men had to catch up with the killers responsible for the atrocities back in the town, for there was nobody else.

The lawman knew that there was only one way to handle their kind.

There might not be any trees to hang the outlaws from in the prairie, but he and his two followers would end this somehow.

Styles had vowed on the blood of the innocents that they would be avenged and he would be the avenger. He urged his mount on and his deputies kept pace.

There was a fury burning in the guts of the veteran lawman and it would not be subdued until he managed to get Dooley and his hired guns in his sights.

The putrid aroma of the gore-stained saloon still lingered in his nostrils. The sight of so much blood haunted Styles as he guided his men through the gloom to a place from which few, if any, had ever returned.

Just like the devilish outlaw leader whom he hunted, Styles had also survived this prairie. The resolute lawman knew how dangerous this unholy place was. He knew how it killed those who entered its unmarked boundaries unprepared.

The prairie showed no mercy.

It destroyed all those who considered themselves invincible. This was no ordinary terrain. Styles felt that it was a conscious entity.

It was a killer more brutal than any living man could ever be. He spurred harder. His deputies followed.

The stars and moon, which had guided them and allowed Styles to follow the outlaws' hoof tracks, were now disappearing in the vast heavens above them. Slowly a storm of unimaginable ferocity was gathering in the sky as it made its way across the untamed land.

Black clouds fought with one another like giants as white flashes lit up the gaps between them. The rumbling of thunder rippled across the prairie ahead of the three lawmen as they continued in their pursuit.

Styles rubbed the grit from his face and glanced briefly up into the sky. His deputies rode beside him and looked to the marshal for guidance. Styles showed no fear and his loyal men trusted his judgement.

They knew that the marshal would never lead them anywhere he was uncertain of. Styles never risked the lives of anyone who rode with him. The hoof tracks had churned up the ground for as far as any of them could see. The lawmen continued to follow the marks in the otherwise undisturbed ground, yet a shadow was starting to spread across it.

'It's getting darn hard to see where these tracks are heading, Bob,' Tyler shouted across to the marshal. 'This storm is moving in fast.'

'I know where they're heading, Jody,' Styles answered, without taking his eyes from the trail they were following.

Hackman closed in on both his comrades. 'But the shadow is covering their tracks up ahead. Pretty soon the wind will kick up the dirt and then we'll not have us anything to follow.'

Styles turned his head towards Hackman.

'Just stick close to me, Ned,' he said. 'I know where them critters are going.'

The deputy was about to ask the marshal where he thought the outlaws were riding to when, suddenly, a bright flash of light defied the darkness and a massive burst of energy exploded in the heavens above them. For a few brief seconds the entire prairie had been lit up as though it were mid-afternoon. Then just as quickly the darkness returned.

As though he had ridden into a wall, Styles hauled back on his reins and stopped his mount.

Tyler and Hackman swung their mounts round and stared back at the troubled marshal. They jabbed their spurs and returned to where he stayed his horse. Both men looked hard into Styles's troubled features as the veteran lawman held his horse in check.

'What's wrong, Bob?' Tyler asked.

'You look like you see a ghost.' Hackman added.

The marshal rubbed his whiskers and glanced at both men in turn.

'Did you see them, boys?' Styles asked.

Hackman moved his skittish mount closer as a deafening thunderclap shook the entire prairie. 'See who?'

'Did you see them killers, Bob?' Tyler asked, vainly trying to steady his mount. 'Is that what you're talking about?'

Styles shook his head and toyed with his reins. 'It weren't the killers I saw, boys.'

His words ate into them with the same ferocity as the night chill. They swung their horses around and looked to where the marshal was gazing.

Neither of them could see anything but the infernal darkness as the storm clouds increased.

'I don't see nothing,' Tyler said.

'Me neither.' Hackman agreed with Tyler. 'Who did you see, Bob?'

The marshal pulled a pipe from his pocket and gripped its stem with his teeth. He chewed on it thoughtfully but made no attempt to light it. His narrowed eyes just kept staring ahead as they awaited the next burst of bright lightning.

'When that burst of lightning spooked us and the horses I swear that I caught a glimpse of riders ahead,' Styles tried to explain.

Tyler removed his hat and rubbed the sweat from his brow with his sleeve. He then replaced it on to his head and tightened the drawstring.

'If you saw riders then it has to be them stinking killers we're chasing,' he said. 'We must be closer to them than we figured, Bob.'

Styles continued to chew on his pipe stem.

'It weren't the killers I saw,' He replied.

Hackman looked at the marshal long and hard. 'How can you be so sure of that, Bob?'

The marshal posed a question.

'How many killers are we hunting?'

'Five,' Tyler answered. 'That's what them folks back in town told us. They said there were five of them and that's how many hoof tracks are carved in this sand.'

'I saw over twenty riders,' Styles said calmly.

'Twenty?' Hackman repeated.

'Are you sure of that, Bob?' Tyler gulped.

'Dead sure.' Styles pulled the pipe from his teeth and pointed with it far ahead to the distant rocks, which were blanketed in darkness. 'I tell you I saw twenty of them, Ned. They were lit up like the Fourth of July. I saw them riding across the top of that damn ridge.'

Neither deputy could see the ridge but both knew that if Styles reckoned he had seen riders then that was exactly what he had done. They felt uneasy.

'I don't like this,' Tyler admitted. 'I don't like this one little bit.'

'Me neither.' Hackman nodded. 'We're risking our damn necks hunting five hardened killers as it is, but I sure don't cotton to running up against twenty varmints.'

Styles continued to stare off into the gloom.

'I caught me a glimpse of twenty or more horsemen and they were headed towards the canyon,' he said. 'I'm just wondering who they are and why they're heading there. They're sure not the *hombres* we're looking for.'

'We don't know that there is a canyon, Bob,' Hackman stated. 'It might just be another tall tale. There's a hundred such stories about this damn prairie.'

Styles looked towards his deputy.

'There's a canyon there OK, Ned,' he said. 'I

know because I chased a varmint all the way there about five years ago. I had to turn back and return to the town 'coz I was running real low on water.'

Hartman shook his head as he considered who the twenty riders might be.

'Were they white men you just seen, Bob?' he wondered. 'Maybe they were troopers. That's gotta be it. You saw a troop of cavalry.'

Styles returned his pipe to his mouth.

'I don't reckon it was troopers. Apart from the killers we're chasing I don't know of any sane white folks that'll risk their necks heading into this place.'

Tyler edged his horse closer to the older man.

'Do you figure it was Injuns?'

Marshal Styles nodded.

'Could be.'

Another violent flash of lightning lit up the land that surrounded them. The deputies drew on their reins and backed away from the apparition they both saw. For a brief moment they too saw the twenty or more horseman riding in single file along the rim of the high rocks.

'I saw them, Bob.' Tyler pointed at the air as darkness again returned. 'Just like you said. There are at least twenty of them.'

'I s-saw the v-varmints as w-well,' Hartman stammered.

Styles steadied his horse.

'We've got four canteens full of water each and enough rations to last us a week,' he said firmly. 'I'm heading on. What do you boys intend doing?'

Despite their fear the deputies both knew that the safest place to be was beside the veteran lawman.

'I'm riding with you, Bob,' Hackman said.

'That goes for me as well,' Tyler added.

The marshal turned his head and called out over his shoulder.

'Then c'mon, boys. We've got us some killers to rope.'

He tapped his spurs and rode towards the distant mountain range.

EIGHT

Hawke hovered over the neck of his horse as he kept the animal moving through the increasing gloom. His eyes continued to search for the strange figure who had saved his bacon and given him the large water bag. There was no sign of Broken Arrow as the drifter forced his stallion on to where he had last espied the raised torches.

The young rider was afraid of the mysterious men he pursued, but something else was also nagging at his guts. Who was Broken Arrow, and why had he not simply killed him? As his tall mount strode across the prairie Hawke felt as though his every move were being watched.

He spurred again and hung on to his reins. The

sound of the approaching storm was growing ever louder and, if for no other reason, Hawke knew he would have to find shelter somewhere ahead. There had to be somewhere that might protect him from the hostile storm, he reckoned. He kept urging his mount on.

Darkness was enveloping the prairie faster than the young horseman could ride. With every beat of his pounding heart he knew that the savage forks of lightning would soon be using him for target practice.

Apart from the towering cactus and the twisted Joshua trees Hawke could not see any protection from the brutal storm. His young eyes widened as another lethal flash erupted in the clouds.

The prairie lit up. Blinding rods of death streaked down from the great storm clouds and struck something far in the distance. A cold shiver traced along the young rider's back as flames burst upwards far off in the distance.

The lightning had found a target.

The dark prairie suddenly had a blazing beacon to light it up.

Hawke leaned over the neck of his horse.

The distant mountains seemed to come no

closer. It was darker now. Stars vanished as the clouds rolled ever closer. The moon had completely disappeared from sight. It was hidden behind a canopy of battling black clouds.

The stench of burning filled the youngster with dread as the horseman tried to ignore the looming danger.

Another massive flash seemed to travel across the clouds as once again streaks of crackling death found their way down into the floor of the prairie.

The expanse of dry terrain shook with the sound of thunder. Nothing created by the hands of mere mortals could ever have equalled such a deafening reverberation of noise.

Hawke rode on. He was too afraid to linger or stop.

There was an urgency in him now. He had to find sanctuary before the storm was overhead.

Again his eyes drifted away from the rocks he was forging towards. He strained to see if the mysterious warrior was somewhere out in the vastness of the prairie, following him.

Broken Arrow had appeared and vanished the day before. He had not shown himself until he had been needed. Like a guardian angel he had simply aided the youngster in his time of need, and then was gone.

Why?

The question still haunted the drifter. Was he still watching? Was Broken Arrow still out there watching, the black pigment still covering his entire body?

Was he keeping pace with the young horseman?

The fearful sound of the rumbling storm echoed all around the rider.

Then, as the heavens yet again illuminated the mountain range for the briefest of moments Hawke suddenly saw the figures riding high across the rim.

Stunned, Hawke drew back on his reins and slowed his stallion. His eyes widened and focused on the riders. The powerful animal kept moving as its young master raised himself in his stirrups.

The open-mouthed drifter could not believe his eyes. These were not the same riders who had been travelling by the light of raised torches, Hawke told himself.

These were different men.

Hawke kept advancing on the wall of jagged rock, his mind racing. These horsemen were at least thirty or more feet higher up from the prairie floor than the men he had espied earlier.

Also they did not have torches.

As the darkness resumed a chilling thought gripped at the very soul of the horseman. He had not counted them but knew that there were at least ten riders moving towards the very place to which he was steering his stallion.

The storm kept growling like a hungry grizzly bear all around him. Terror engulfed the drifter. He drew rein and looked heavenward at the angry dark sky. The flashes of lightning were miles away from where he held his stallion in check, and yet he knew the streaks of white death were getting closer.

Explosions seemed to be everywhere. The only certainty was that they were heading towards him with increasing speed.

Hawke rubbed the sweat from his face along his sleeve and swung the horse full circle, desperately trying to see if there were any safe places closer than the rocks.

No matter how hard he looked Hawke could not see anything that offered him or his stallion refuge from what was approaching like a mighty locomotive thundering across the open prairie towards him.

He cursed and steadied his skittish mount.

There was nothing he could do except continue on his present course towards the place where he had seen the fiery torches, even though that meant heading towards the line of riders who were navigating the rim.

Hawke swung his mount and spurred hard. The stallion galloped through the tumbleweed and sagebrush towards the unknown.

Hawke gripped his saddle horn with one hand and his reins with the other. He was now racing towards the high mountains and the strange black mountains at renewed speed.

The horse was just as scared as its master but it knew that when danger was close you galloped as fast as your legs could take you.

The stallion weaved its way through the maze of twisted cactus and Joshua trees, trying to get off the prairie before the devastating lightning struck. Hawke whipped his reins across the tail of his mount and urged the wide-eyed creature on. The scent of burning filled the drifter's nostrils as more and more lightning splintered through the night. Hawke encouraged the distraught horse to find a pace that it had never found before. Again Hawke glanced up at the storm.

It was getting more and more violent.

He guided the stallion down into a deep gully and drove his spurs into its flanks. The terrified creature used its powerful muscles to carry its rider up the opposite side of the incline, emerging back on to the flat prairie floor.

It leapt over clumps of sagebrush and then charged back across the dusty ground. Hawke could feel the flesh on his back tingling as another deafening thunderclap exploded in the hostile sky.

Hawke narrowed his eyes as more flashes of nature's venom momentarily turned the blackness into blinding light. He knew that to remain here in the exposed prairie was to await death as surely as a condemned man awaits the hangman's noose.

The prairie was burning all around the young rider. Wherever he glanced he could see fire rising from the withered vegetation. Then another fork of lightning crackled through the air and struck a mighty cactus.

It was like watching a stick of dynamite exploding. Hawke dragged his mount to his left, attempting to avoid the long, sharp thorns that flew in all directions.

As his stallion kept forging on, Hawke wondered about the horsemen. Where had they gone?

Hawke spurred hard. Then, as his sturdy mount gained speed, a sudden sight greeted him between the lightning flashes.

The galloping stallion had only just negotiated its way between two giant Joshua trees when an ominous black form appeared directly ahead. Whatever it was it was blocking his horse's path.

Hawke had little time to react.

Frantically he fumbled with his long leathers, hauled rein and brought his horse to an abrupt halt before it could crash into the unexpected obstruction. A cloud of dust spewed out from beneath the animal's hoofs as they dug deep into the soft dirt. Its master fought to remain in his saddle.

Hawke was thrown forward. He barely had time to grab at his horse's neck to prevent himself from being unseated. Looking lke a rag doll, Hawke hung on to the bridle of his mount.

Dust smothered the rider, choking in its density.

Hawke had not had time to see what it was that had stopped his advance. All he knew for sure was that he had nearly ridden the stallion into something as dark as the prairie itself.

The dust began to clear.

Awkwardly, Hawke placed a hand on the mane of the skittish stallion and pushed himself back in the saddle. He steadied himself and tried to focus his gaze through the eerie darkness.

Hawke gasped and stared ahead.

It moved forward towards Hawke like a bad omen. The black stallion with its similarly dark rider walked through the dust straight for the startled Hawke. The drifter swallowed hard and stared at the unearthly face as it closed in on him. Its haunting unblinking eyes were the only feature of the painted face that confirmed its humanity.

A raised hand showed Hawke its palm.

Hawke steadied his mount as it tried to shy.

'Broken Arrow!' Hawke gasped, suddenly recognizing his benefactor.

There was not a sound from the figure. Broken Arrow continued to allow his mount to close the distance between the two horsemen. The drifter stared at him in wonderment, watching as he pulled back on his crude leathers and stopped the stallion.

Hawke summoned all of his resolve.

'Why have you stopped me?' Hawke asked.

Broken Arrow remained as mute as at the previous

time when they had encountered one another. He turned and pointed to the distant mountains, then shook his head. For a reason known only to him, Broken Arrow did not wish Hawke to continue. He waved his hands above the unkempt mane of his stallion.

Hawke glanced at the storm clouds. Then he looked back at the dark face of the Indian.

'I get the feeling that you don't want me to carry on towards the mountains, but there ain't no way I'm staying here, not with that damn storm coming,' Hawke shouted. He gathered up his reins and steered his mount around the silent Broken Arrow.

The Indian's dark arm reached out and pressed into the drifter's chest. The two men's eyes locked. If eyes could speak then Broken Arrow was telling Hawke not to proceed.

'I'm headed there, friend,' Hawke insisted. 'I don't hanker to get myself hit by that lightning. You can come with me or stay here.'

Broken Arrow knew that there was no point in trying to stop the nervous drifter. He lowered his arm and rested it on the shoulders of his horse. Silently he dragged his reins to his right and nodded to Hawke.

Hawke spurred and continued his race to reach the mountain range before the storm caught up with and destroyed them both. As the drifter raced astride his stallion he could hear Broken Arrow keeping pace with his mount's every stride.

NINE

Like a troop of demonic killers, more akin to the denizens of Hell than of the desolate region they were travelling through, the five ruthless outlaws had made good progress through the narrow canyon towards their goal. They had nearly reached their destination when suddenly one of the storm's most vicious lightning forks struck at the very rim of the canyon's jagged walls high above them. Stunned by the sudden explosion the horsemen stopped their mounts and looked upwards. An avalanche of smouldering rocks came crashing from the rim above.

Dooley stood defiantly in his stirrups, holding his horse in check. His narrowed eyes watched the debris falling down over the rough sides of the canyon before it showered over the outlaws.

Rocks and dust crashed to the floor of the canyon as Dooley steadied his mount. He fixedly watched the others as they gripped their reins in fear.

He said nothing.

Then, as though nothing had happened, the outlaw leader waved his followers on. The four riders nervously drove their mounts past their watchful trail finder. As the last of his men thundered by him Dooley swung his mount and followed.

The canyon was getting narrower the further they rode into its depths.

'Keep them horses going, boys.' Dooley bellowed out his orders as the sound of the lightning strike echoed around them. 'We ain't got far to go before we reach the mission.'

'If we reach it,' Landon said.

Chandler turned as Dooley caught up with him.

'The storm's getting mighty bad, Sheb,' he yelled as debris scattered down over them. 'I sure hope that you're right.'

Dooley said nothing. He spurred and rode ahead of his men, not slowing his pace. He continued to lead the riders through the eerie light towards the place that he imagined only he knew of.

Landon kept looking up at the continuing storm. Streaks of energy lit up the battling clouds. Each time a deafening noise shook the canyon around them the outlaws looked up.

'I don't like this,' Landon admitted as he rode close to Reece and Janson. 'Nope, I don't like this one bit.'

Eb Reece gave a nod.

'Me neither, but just think of the treasure that's waiting for us, Joe,' he grunted, then spurred hard after Dooley. 'Pretty soon we'll be as rich as kings.'

Yet no amount of potential treasure could quell the fear each of the horsemen had burning in his guts. They had all witnessed the power of a single lightning strike as it carved a path down from the storm clouds and turned solid rock into fragments. Each of the outlaws knew that they were dealing with something beyond their comprehension. This was no normal enterprise they had embarked upon, they all silently thought. This was potentially the most dangerous venture any of them had ever tackled. Yet their greed outweighed their combined fear.

Landon bit his lip and continued to trail Dooley. Then his narrowed eyes espied something he had not expected to see, high above them.

Frantically Landon punched Janson on the arm and then pointed upward at the rim of the canyon. His finger jabbed at the air.

'Look up there, Poke,' Landon shouted.

Poke Janson looked up. As the lightning flashes ceased to dazzle the rider also saw what his cohort was pointing at. A cold chill traced along his spine.

'Holy cow!' he exclaimed in stunned surprise. 'I see 'em. We ain't alone, Joe.'

The line of more than a dozen horsemen could be clearly seen as they steered their mounts along the jagged rim of the canyon. There was no defining shape to any of the horsemen. The only thing the outlaws could make out clearly was their silhouettes. They were quite enough to trouble the outlaws.

It was obvious that whoever these riders were, they too were following a parallel route along the canyon.

'Do you see them?' Landon called out.

'I see them, Joe.' Janson whipped the long ends of his reins and thundered towards Dooley.

Dooley heard the sound of the outlaw's horse's hoofs beating on the canyon floor behind him. He stopped his mount and swung his horse around just as the wide-eyed outlaw drew up beside him. He was puzzled as to why the rider was aiming his finger at the high canyon rim.

'What in tarnation is eating at you?' Dooley snapped.

'Look up yonder, Sheb,' Janson yelled out as the others caught up with them. 'We got us company.'

Undisturbed, Dooley coolly leaned back and looked to where his men were pointing. The sight of many riders greeted his eyes. Dooley shook his head and spat at the ground.

'You're right. It looks like we got us some unexpected visitors, boys,' Dooley drawled. He pulled a cigar from his pocket and bit off its tip. 'And the last thing we need is folks tagging along.'

'Who are they, Sheb?' Reece asked. Dooley rammed his cigar between his lips.

'Damned if I know,' Dooley struck a match and cupped its flame to the end of his cigar. He puffed feverishly, then blew smoke at the unburned remainder of his match. 'There sure are a lot of them, though.'

85

'Let's get out of here.' Landon suggested, rubbing the sweat from his face with the tails of his bandanna.

'Joe's right,' Chandler agreed with his fellow outlaw. 'We oughta turn and ride.'

'I got me a feeling that they're bandits out to let us do all the digging and when we haul the treasure out of the ground they'll kill us,' Janson opined.

'Joe might be right, Sheb,' Reece agreed. 'The safest place for to be ain't here.'

Dooley stared at his nervous gang through the smoke that flowed through his lips. He shook his head as he continued to watch the line of mysterious horsemen.

'Listen to yourselves, boys.' He mocked them like a father taunting his children. 'You sound like a bunch of old women. You see a herd of riders and you want to quit. You want to high-tail it just coz there's a line of riders watching us?'

'It ain't safe here,' Janson said. 'Them riders could pick us off real easy from up there. We'd be sitting ducks.'

'It'd be a damn turkey shoot and we'd be the damn turkeys, Sheb,' Chandler agreed.

Dooley pulled the cigar from his mouth and

tapped its ash at the ground. His eyes remained on the horsemen far above the canyon.

'I'm not scared of them critters even if you boys are,' Dooley said. 'We've come all this way, we're within five minutes of getting our hands on the treasure and you want to quit. It don't figure.'

Landon eased his horse close to their leader.

'We don't know who them varmints are, Sheb. They might be waiting for us to find the gold and then they'll wipe us out,' the nervous outlaw suggested.

Dooley replaced the cigar between his teeth. He continued to study the horsemen while the storm raged on above them. It was like listening to dynamite sticks exploding, yet the outlaw leader did not flinch.

'Who do you figure they are, Eb?' he asked Reece.

Reece stared up. 'I reckon they're bandits. We're mighty close to the border. Bandits roam all over. They're gonna let us find the gold and then strike.'

'They ain't bandits,' Dooley disagreed.

'Then what are they?'

There was a long pause while Dooley continued to watch the horsemen, who had stopped their progress on the high rim of the canyon and were watching the five outlaws who stared up at them.

'Injuns,' Dooley said through a cloud of cigar smoke. He hauled both his guns from their holsters and cocked them. He raised his weaponry, aimed and fired.

Clouds encircled the barrels of his guns.

The reports of the deafening shots equalled the roar of the storm that raged far above them. The two bullets tore up through the eerie light and hit two of the mysterious horsemen.

The outlaws around Dooley watched in stunned awe as his shots plucked the riders from their mounts. Within seconds the rest of the strange horsemen had vanished from view.

Dooley gave out a satisfied grunt, lowered his smoking guns and poked them back into his holsters.

He glanced at Reece and the rest of his gang. A twisted grin appeared etched across his hardened features.

'I should have said "dead Injuns", boys.' He laughed before gathering up his loose reins and swinging his mount around. He drove his spurs into the flesh of his animal. 'C'mon. They won't give us any trouble now.'

The smell of gunsmoke filled the nostrils of the four outlaws. They had never seen anyone who could handle his weaponry as skilfully as Dooley. That was why he was the leader of the gang.

None of them wanted him to turn his guns in their direction. Dooley was far more dangerous than anyone else they had ever encountered.

One by one the four outlaws turned their horses and jabbed their spurs. Dust was kicked up from their horses' hoofs as the men chased Dooley.

The four outlaws trailed Dooley as he led them through the canyon towards the mission. Dooley inhaled deeply on the cigar between his teeth. He knew they were now close to the fortune he had promised them. A fortune which, it seemed, only they knew about.

Nobody was going to stand between him and the fortune he believed lay somewhere within the remnants of the mission's walls.

A treasure-trove which, Dooley believed, had his name upon it.

TEN

Hawke hauled leather and stopped his stallion at the mouth of the canyon. The young drifter could feel the hairs on his neck standing up as Broken Arrow trailed him into the canyon. The sound of Dooley's shots still echoed like an ominous warning of what they could expect should they continue. Hawke turned to look back at his heavily disguised companion.

Why had Broken Arrow not wanted to him to enter the canyon? The question kept nagging at the youngster as he slowly turned his mount and looked at his silent companion.

What danger was there hidden in the canyon,

which even the seemingly fearless Broken Arrow was wary of? Hawke stared at the dark rider.

No matter how many times Hawke cast his eyes upon Broken Arrow, he could not get used to the horrific appearance. In his most frightening of nightmares he had never conjured up anything that looked remotely like Broken Arrow. To have set eyes upon the man had shocked Hawke and he was still unable to rid himself of that feeling.

The storm erupted across the prairie again. The flashing illumination of the lightning lit up the strange creature who now rode with Hawke. The feathered war bonnet seemed to be alive as the storm's breeze moved the black wings above its owner's head.

Hawke steadied his stallion and approached his silent companion. However, the Indian seemed to be totally unaware of him. Broken Arrow seemed to be quite transfixed by the sight of the rocks of the canyon walls. It was as though he were looking for something, Hawke thought.

But what?

'Now we're here I got me a feeling that you might just be right, Broken Arrow,' Hawke said. He sighed heavily. 'This canyon ain't no safer than it is back there on the prairie. In fact it might be a whole lot more dangerous.'

Broken Arrow remained silent. Either he did not hear or he simply did not understand. He sat astride his black stallion and stared at the towering canyon sides.

Hawke wondered about the shooting they had heard. Then he saw the discarded torches on the ground. He moved his mount close to them, feeling uneasy. He looked all around them as yet more splinters of lightning carved a jagged route down from the battling clouds towards the ground. A huge cactus less than a hundred feet from where they rested upon their mounts took the full force of the lightning and disintegrated into a fiery blaze.

The sheer power of the strike left nothing but smouldering ashes in its wake.

'Yep, I reckon you were right. This place is mighty dangerous.' Hawke gulped as he stared out at the remains of the blazing cactus. 'I got me a feeling you might be a lot wiser than I first figured.'

With Hawke trailing his every move, Broken Arrow swung his stallion around and rode to the opposite side of the canyon. He began to studying the canyon wall with the same intensity that he had given to the other rock face.

'What are you looking for?' Hawke asked as the storm grew even more violent. His young eyes glanced up at the heavens nervously. 'Whatever it is I sure hope you find it real fast, Broken Arrow. I got me a feeling that lightning ain't gonna keep missing us for much longer.'

Broken Arrow heeled his powerful stallion to pace around the mouth of the canyon as he studied its rugged walls even more closely. Hawke had no idea what Broken Arrow was searching for but he prayed the Indian would find it quickly.

Several streaks of lightning crackled along the edge of the canyon wall. Hawke gripped his reins tightly and kept his terrified horse in check.

'What the hell are you looking for, *amigo*?' Hawke asked as the ground beneath their horses' hoofs shook violently. The youngster fought with his mount when another clap of deafening thunder spooked both horse and rider. The drifter glanced up at his companion and was stunned to see that neither Broken Arrow nor his mount reacted to the explosive noise.

Hawke steadied his horse.

He was about to speak when Broken Arrow pointed a finger at the canyon wall. Hawke tapped his spurs and edged his horse to close the distance between them. He looked to where Broken Arrow was indicating. The rugged rocks were shrouded in a mass of shadows and revealed no clue as to what the Indian seemed to be pointing his bow at.

'What in tarnation have you seen, Broken Arrow?' Hawke asked. 'Because I sure don't see anything except a lot of boulders.'

The painted face turned towards him with a look of surprise. Lightning flashed across Broken Arrow's features. The eyes of the Indian seemed to shine brightly amid the dark pigment which obscured his other lineaments. Hawke shook his head as he struggled again to understand what his companion had spotted.

'What's got you so all fired up?' Hawke asked again.

Broken Arrow pointed again at rocks about ten feet up from the floor of the canyon. He watched as the young drifter screwed up his eyes and studied the rocks more closely.

At last Hawke caught a glimpse of what his companion was indicating. The boulders had concealed a well-hidden crevice in the rocks.

'I see it!' he exclaimed.

Broken Arrow gave a firm nod of his head, then gripped the sides of his horse with his moccasins. He tapped his black stallion's tail with his bow. The black stallion obeyed its master and charged forward. It began to climb the seemingly impossible slope.

'Where you going, Broken Arrow?' Hawke called out as he watched his companion.

The silent Indian rode the powerful stallion expertly up the side of the canyon wall towards the natural crack in the rocks.

Hawke watched open-mouthed as the Indian somehow encouraged the stallion over the loose surface towards his goal. The drifter had never before seen such a large horse move as sure-footedly as a mountain goat.

Broken Arrow continued to urge his mount up the rugged slope until he reached the barely visible ledge. The intrepid rider stopped his mount and signalled down to the astonished Hawke.

Dumbfounded, Hawke stared up to where Broken Arrow rested upon his black stallion. From where he sat astride his own mount he could barely see the ledge. Yet there had to be one, he reasoned. The dark warrior waved his arm at the drifter again.

Hawke knew that Broken Arrow wanted him to follow.

The youngster gritted his teeth and held his reins firmly in his gloved hands. He knew that the climb was possible even though he still did not believe. He spurred his mount and held on with all his might as it started to ascend the steep slope to where Broken Arrow sat silently watching.

'Keep going, boy,' Hawke urged his mount as its forelegs pawed at the surface of the slope. 'You can make it if that black horse made it.'

The stallion continued to press its hoofs into the friable gravel and to force itself up the rugged slope. Hawke wondered if it was strong enough to carry both the hefty water bag and himself up the steep incline.

The drifter thought about Broken Arrow, who was watching his every movement. The Indian was riding bareback, which meant his mount had had far less weight to carry up the slope.

It was far too late to be worried about that, though. The youngster was already halfway up the side of the canyon wall and could not quit now.

He had to continue.

Loose stones slipped from under the stallion's hoofs, yet the courageous horse continued to obey its master and climb up to where Broken Arrow awaited.

Then a deafening thunderclap shook the ground, enough to dislodge great lumps of rock. Hawke watched helplessly as rocks of all sizes rolled down the slope like a dry avalanche. A few moments later a flash of blinding light lit up the canyon. Hawke balanced in his stirrups and hung on.

The exhausted horse drew itself up on to the ridge beside Broken Arrow and hung its head. It snorted as it tried to catch its breath. Hawke was as breathless as his mount. He straightened up on his saddle and stared at the cleft in the rocks. He looked at the Indian. There was no sign of any emotion in the painted face.

Broken Arrow then hauled his crude reins away from the edge of the steep drop until his horse was facing the fissure.

'A tunnel?' Hawke gasped as he suddenly saw what his companion was facing. 'You darn found a tunnel, Broken Arrow. Where does it go?'

There was no reply from the warrior. He just tilted his head backwards and stared up at the storm. Broken Arrow knew that the narrow ledge he and the young drifter were perched upon was no safer than the canyon floor when deadly shafts of lightning were hitting anything the gods chose to attack.

The acrid aroma of sulphur filled both men's nostrils as a new, more intense battle erupted across the heavens. The warrior lowered his head and glared at the nervous Hawke. Their eyes met and somehow the drifter seemed to know exactly what Broken Arrow was thinking. Hawke seemed to trust the eyes that glowed in the continual flashes of lightning.

Broken Arrow waved his bow in the air and tapped the flanks of his powerful mount with his moccasins. The night sky was now almost white as electrical energy pulsated above them to the reverberating beat of Heaven's war drums.

Hawke watched as Broken Arrow signalled to him. The drifter watched as his companion slapped his bow across the tail of his stallion and rode into the darkness.

Hawke pulled his horse's head up with his reins

and allowed the animal to carefully negotiate the ledge towards the tunnel. He swallowed hard and did the only thing he could do.

He followed.

ELEVEN

For longer than anyone could recall there had been stories of a reclusive tribe who lived on the prairie, yet in all that time no living soul had ever seen them. Unlike most tall tales the stories concerning these reclusive creatures were all true. There was indeed a strange race of nomadic people who roamed the vast prairie, which spanned both sides of the border. Like living ghosts they moved unseen in the most dangerous and hostile of terrains keeping away from the outside world and the men from whom they desired to remain apart.

They lived and died without ever leaving a trace. In the land they occupied it was easy to return to dust. They built no temples for, unlike many other men, they had no desire to prove their existence.

Since time itself began, it seemed, they had simply existed.

Long before other tribes had been evicted from their ancestral lands by the white intruders they had roamed through the parched land knowing where they could find water to drink and food to eat.

Unlike the other tribes these people had never had any roots anywhere. They had always moved with the seasons and they followed the once abundant buffalo. At one time they themselves had been as abundant as the buffalo and, just like the huge animals, they too had diminished in numbers.

When the buffalo had been virtually wiped out the same fate befell the nomads who had relied so heavily upon them. There was an old saying in the lodges of many natives: that everything is joined together and when the coyote dies so does the wolf.

Even though they had managed to keep their existence a secret that had not been enough to protect them. Without the buffalo and other game to nourish their women and children the tribe had declined drastically to a point of no return.

It had only taken a generation to reduce them to just over a dozen aged warriors. Dooley's ruthless shots had taken two more of them in the blink of an eye.

These Indians had never called anywhere home, but for those who remained the canyon had always been considered a holy place. The mission had failed a century earlier because they believed their Great Spirit was unwilling to share the holy shrine with another deity.

The dumbfounded warriors looked at their dead on the rim of the canyon. Their blood glistened in the light of the storm as the remaining braves cautiously moved back to where the bodies lay.

The horror of the sight confused and angered those who remained of the ghost riders.

The two deadly shots which Dooley had fired up from the canyon still resonated in the ears of the eleven warriors. Fate had been cruel to them for decades but this murderous act had fuelled their anger.

They watched as the five outlaws rode off into the depths of the canyon towards the mission. Then they moved to recover the bodies of their two dead braves.

For countless years the tribesmen had lived in

peace and managed to avoid all contact with the outside world. Now everything had changed. For the first time it was neither hunger nor illness that had claimed two of their tribe. It was white men who had mindlessly killed them. Suddenly the remnants of the elusive nomadic tribe had seen two of their number slain for reasons they could not comprehend.

Now bewilderment turned to something else. It turned into anger and the thirst for revenge.

Centuries of peaceful existence had been destroyed in seconds by two small pellets of lethal lead. The two pitiful bodies lay where they had fallen from their ponies upon the jagged rim of the canyon. Pools of gore surrounded them both and ran freely down the craggy slope.

The last of the nomadic warriors vowed that the bullets that had extinguished the lives of their brothers could not go unchallenged.

Most men as long-lived as they might have reasoned that they were simply too old to fight the outlaws. They had only the weapons of their ancestors, unlike the five heavily armed riders, and there were no young bucks left to fight.

All of their young men had gone.

Time had already taken them as it had taken their womenfolk and children. The aged braves who remained had nothing to lose but their lives.

It was a price they were all willing to pay.

All those who remained of a once proud race were old and ready to die in order to seek retribution. For no matter how old a man becomes he is still a man.

The warriors looked at one another as the storm raged overhead. They knew without talking what had to be done and were willing to do it. They wrapped the limp bodies of their dead in the blankets from the backs of their ponies as was their custom, and they looked out from their high vantage point.

Unaware of the avenging eyes that were watching the outlaws' progress, Dooley and his men continued riding towards the mission. They were still intent on finding the treasure they believed to be there, and they would not be easily swayed from their purpose.

Standing like withered trees upon the high canyon rim, the last few of the mysterious tribesmen knew where the devilish riders were heading.

Dooley and his men were riding to the mission.

One of the warriors raised his bloody hands, as if beckoning to the thunder gods for the strength he knew he and his fellow tribesmen needed. As the storm charged the air around them with electricity the warrior smeared the blood in vivid red lines across his cheeks.

He then plucked his lance from off his pony and aimed it down into the canyon at the riders. Soon all the old tribesmen were standing on the edge of the rim, holding their crude weapons above their heads in defiance of the lethal storm that raged around them.

The valiant brave began to chant a haunting tune. It challenged the noise of the deadly storm. Soon each of the secretive Indians was also chanting their unearthly song.

The strange sound of the ancient hymn rang down from their vantage point. It followed the outlaws through the twisting canyon like a sidewinder seeking its prey.

It was the song of the dead.

TWELVE

Clouds of choking dust spiralled up from the floor of the canyon as gusts of wind swept through its winding length. They rose up into the unsettled sky far above the rim of the canyon as storm clouds continued to collide with one another. For a while there was nothing but a wall of blinding grit across the width of the canyon. The five outlaws were advancing into the unknown, but nothing could deter them now. They could sense that they were getting closer with each faltering step of their horses' hoofs.

Dooley chewed on the grit that tried to whip him into submission. He lowered his head and kept spurring his horse forward.

Lesser men might have panicked and given up

their quest, but Dooley would never quit. Greed was dragging him ever onward and his gang determinedly followed.

The flash lightning and the earth-shaking rumble of thunder told the five ruthless horsemen that they were still on course and nearing their goal. Any thought about the innocent dead whom they had left in their wake vanished as the gusting dirt began to ease. Shafts of electrical light lured the riders on and Dooley ensured that they would follow or find themselves dead.

Every sinew in his body told Dooley that they were now close to their destination. Tantalizing glimpses of the bell tower appeared to the ruthless outlaw.

Dooley drove his mount through the last of the choking dust and shook the same from his face. Then, at last, he saw the unmistakable tower clearly.

The leader of the gang reined in as his raw eyes espied the reason for his returning to this deadly place. Dooley slowed his horse as it advanced on the ruins of the mission.

'There it is, boys,' Dooley yelled out triumphantly. 'I told you I'd get us here.'

Its once high adobe walls had been crumbling for

a hundred years, yet it was still possible to see what it had once been. The bell tower still dominated the ruins. Its bells had long since fallen from the rotten wooden frame that had held them in place.

They lay half-buried in the sand, looking like giant tombstones.

Yet it was the tower that had guided Dooley to the still crystal-clear springwater on his last visit. Like a lighthouse above hidden rocks it signalled where the spring of pure water could be found. In this forsaken terrain water was more precious than the gold for which Dooley had returned.

The deadly outlaw led his four companions towards the tower slowly and surely. He rubbed the sand from his eyes and looked around the ruins of the once dominant mission.

The five outlaws rode up to what remained of the mission and the high bell tower. The storm still raged in the vast sky, and yet none of the horsemen noticed. All any of them could think about was the treasure that Dooley had assured them they would find somewhere amongst its ruins.

They dismounted next to what appeared to be the only wall remaining intact.

Landon looked around them. He muttered

quietly, 'I don't see any gold.'

'Hush up, you fool,' Reece warned. He glanced at Dooley before returning his attention to the outlaw. 'Sheb will kill you if he hears you bad-mouthing.'

Dooley looked at the sand piled up against the walls.

'I told you I'd get you here, boys,' he said. He led his mount round the wall they would use as a wind-break. 'When the storm passes and the sun rises we'll start looking for the fortune, boys.'

Reece followed, his mount in tow. 'The hard bit is getting away from here, Sheb. This ain't the best place to start digging for gold.'

'This is where I found me the trinkets, Eb,' Dooley said, securing his mount. 'Gold trinkets. I tell you there's a fortune buried here and it's waiting for us to dig it up.'

Janson, Chandler and Landon all led their horses, following Dooley and Reece. They remained quiet as the lightning flashed up in the heavens. They stayed close to the wall, knowing that when lightning struck men had a habit of dying.

Dooley secured his horse and unsaddled it.

'Don't none of you start fretting,' Dooley said. He bit the end off another of his cigars and gripped its length between his teeth. 'When we ride away from this old mission we'll be richer than one of them kings back in the old country.'

Reece dragged his saddle off his horse's back and dropped it against the wall.

'I don't mind being rich as long as I'm still alive,' he said, then spat.

Dooley eyed Reece. 'The storm ain't nothing to be troubled about.'

'It ain't the storm I'm talking about,' Reece argued. 'I'm talking about them Injuns. If they attack us here we ain't got a lot of cover.'

'They've gone,' Dooley told him, and grinned.

Landon stopped walking. The storm was unlike anything he had ever experienced before. He had never seen a sky so alive with so much power before.

'What time is it?' he asked as he tied his reins around a large sod brick.

Janson pulled out a pocket watch and opened its lid. He stared at its dial, then raised it to his ear.

'I must have forgotten to wind the damn thing,' he wailed, then he sighed.

Landon looked at the others.

'Don't any of you know what time it is?'

Dooley struck a match and cupped its flame

against the wind. He sucked its flame into the cigar and exhaled a line of smoke.

'How come you're so interested in the time, Joe?' he asked, laughing loudly. 'You got a date with a bar girl?'

Landon kept looking at the sky. Beads of sweat made trails down his face through the thick dirt that covered his features. The thing disturbing Landon was that it seemed to be as light as midday and yet he knew that it was the middle of the night.

He mistrusted his own senses.

'I ain't so sure it's still night, Sheb,' Landon said. 'I ain't never seen night-time as light as this.'

Dooley pulled his own watch from his vest pocket and flicked its lid open. He stared at it, then looked at Landon.

'It's gone midnight, Joe,' he said.

'Midnight?' Landon repeated in disbelief. 'How can that be?'

'It's this damn storm, Joe.' Chandler spat as he pulled his saddle from the back of his own mount and laid it next to the others. 'It's kinda eerie and no mistake.'

Dooley walked to the rest of his men.

'Rub down your horses, boys,' he ordered. 'Feed

and water them while I rustle up a fire to cook us some vittles. Reckon we all deserve some ham and beans.'

The men nodded like faithful hounds. No matter how violent the storm might become it was Dooley whom they really feared. He was far more dangerous and unpredictable than mere lightning. They had seen him single-handedly kill a dozen men back in the nameless town. They had also witnessed his unholy accuracy when he had slain the two Indians on the canyon rim. Dooley was a man none of them dared rile. Each of them knew the penalty for doing that.

THIRTEEN

The line of riders blended into the weathered rocks as they silently made the steep descent into the canyon. There was little difference in their bleached hue from that of the ground beneath their ponies unshod hoofs. All eleven of the warriors were silent as they fearlessly steered their mounts down from the high rim into the belly of the canyon.

They had ceased the chanting to the gods. Now only the storm resounded across the prairie and the canyon. Their aged eyes looked out from their colourless faces to where the bell tower at San Angelo awaited.

The sky was the colour of molten silver. Lightning

continued to streak among the clouds as the riders allowed their mounts to find their own route down into the perilous canyon, as they had done for years.

The nomadic tribe had once prospered in this land. Now they simply existed. Each of them knew that they were riding towards their own doom, yet they kept encouraging their thin ponies ever downward into the canyon.

They were destined to fight, perhaps to die.

Perhaps both.

Like mysterious phantoms the silver-haired figures looked more like skeletons than living men, but they doggedly continued to ride down towards the floor of the canyon. In contrast to the heavily armed outlaws whom they sought, their only weapons were small bows and quivers filled with flint-tipped arrows.

Yet they were unafraid.

There was nothing left to live for.

They were ready to kill. They were also ready to die.

FOURTEEN

The three lawmen drove their mounts through the sagebrush towards the mouth of the canyon. Marshal Styles had used his skill as a tracker to trail the five outlaws across the prairie to the start of the canyon. Styles lifted an arm and stopped his deputies beneath the high jagged walls of sheer rock. He dragged his horse back and stared at the churned-up ground. Tyler and Hackman watched as the experienced lawman steadied his horse and looked down at the hoof-tracks that had brought him to this ominous place.

'What's wrong, Bob?' Tyler asked the marshal.

Styles slowly lowered himself from his saddle. He held on to his reins with one hand and knelt down.

He studied the ground the way some men study books. There was a story to be read in the churned-up sand and he was one of the few men capable of reading it.

'Something's wrong,' Styles said, apparently mystified. 'I ain't too sure what but something don't figure.'

Both the deputies looked down at the marshal as his gloved hand hovered over the hoof-tracks. They had never seen Styles look so puzzled before.

'What you seen, Bob?' Tyler asked.

'Have you noticed something?' Hackman added.

Styles looked up at both of his deputies, then rose to his full height. He toyed with his reins and stared at the sky. The storm seemed to be far worse deep into the long winding canyon. He turned and strode carefully back to where his trusted men sat astride their mounts. With each step his eyes studied the sand.

'What do the tracks tell you, Bob?' Tyler wondered.

Styles led his mount closer to his men. He rested a hand on the saddle horn and paused. He walked around the horses and looked at the canyon walls, then returned to his mount.

'Tell us, Bob,' Hackman pressed. 'What do the tracks tell you?'

'That's the problem,' Styles answered. He lifted his left leg and poked his boot into the stirrup. 'The tracks kinda tell me a whole heap of things.'

The deputies watched as the marshal mounted his horse in one easy action.

'But you can read them, Bob. Right?' Hackman pressed again. 'You can always read tracks.'

Tyler noticed the confused expression on Styles's face. He edged his horse closer to the marshal.

'What is it, Bob?' he asked. 'What's eating at you?'

Styles raised his head and looked hard into both men's faces. He tightened his drawstring and sighed.

'Them hoof-tracks are telling me something that I don't understand, boys,' he admitted. 'I trailed the five killers to this very spot as easy as spit, but something just don't figure.'

Hackman leaned closer. 'What don't figure?'

'The ground is mighty cut up but there seems to be two new horses' hoof-tracks there.' Styles answered, pointing at the disturbed sand. 'There are two sets of tracks that I ain't seen before.'

'Two new sets of tracks?' Tyler repeated. 'How

can that be, Bob?'

Styles stared at the ground. He shook his head.

'Two riders came in from the heart of the prairie,' the marshal explained. 'Their tracks are fresher than the ones left by the five killers we're chasing. That means they got here a lot later.'

'Two riders came from the heart of the prairie?' Tyler was as confused as his question indicated. 'How can anyone survive out there?'

Hackman interrupted, 'So two other varmints followed the killers? Maybe they joined up with the bunch we're following.'

Marshal Styles looked at his deputy.

'You don't understand, Ned. Two horsemen rode out of the prairie. One of them is a white man. The other must be an Injun because he's riding an unshod horse.'

'Maybe the Injun was following this rider,' Tyler suggested.

Styles shook his head. 'Nope. They rode together, Jody.'

'That's kinda unusual.' Hackman shrugged. 'They arrived after the killers, you say? That means they're following them into the canyon, just like we're gonna do.'

'Wrong again, Ned.' Styles sighed heavily.

'The killers headed into the canyon though. Right?' Tyler asked the marshal.

Marshal Styles pointed down the canyon. 'That's right. They headed into this damn canyon, Jody. All five of them went thataway.'

'How come you still look confused, Bob?' Tyler pulled out his tobacco pouch and started to make himself a smoke.

The marshal gathered up his reins. In all the years he had read the tracks of those he hunted, the disturbed sand was telling him something that seemed impossible.

'The two other riders seem to have just vanished into thin air,' Styles said.

'That ain't possible.' Tyler gasped. 'Nobody just vanishes into thin air.'

'Them two riders sure did,' Styles insisted.

'But where did they go?' Hackman wondered.

Marshal Styles grunted as his eyes vainly searched for answers. Yet no matter how hard he tried the lawman could not see where Hawke and Broken Arrow had gone.

'I don't know. That's what's puzzling me.'

The three troubled lawmen resumed their hunt

and started down into the depths of the canyon. They were headed to where the storm still raged: toward the flashing sky and the sound of clouds colliding.

Without even realizing it they were spurring towards something far more dangerous than any of them had ever encountered before.

Styles and his loyal deputies knew that they were riding headlong towards a tempest.

They did not slow their pace.

FIFTEEN

The answer to the question that puzzled the three lawmen was simple. The two riders who had mysteriously vanished at the mouth of the canyon were riding due south through the natural tunnel that ran deep in one of the canyon walls. For what had seemed like an eternity the two very different horsemen had moved unseen and unheard through the unknown tunnel. The young drifter had followed his shadowy guide like a faithful hound. Hawke had no idea why Broken Arrow was taking this unexpected route, or where they would find themselves when it ended. All Hawke knew for sure was that he trusted his companion.

Broken Arrow drew back on his reins and

stopped his stallion. His narrowed eyes stared along the tunnel towards the small dot of light far ahead of them.

Suddenly bats came racing through the long tunnel from behind them. Both riders felt the slight breeze as the creatures glided expertly through their domain.

Hawke drew level with his mysterious benefactor and scout. The drifter looked all around them as he nervously steadied his mount.

They had followed the tunnel for more than two miles before they reaching this spot. Their journey had been so long that their eyes had adjusted to the darkness. Hawke rested his mount and glared ahead to where Broken Arrow's gaze was fixed upon the small light.

Hawke wondered why Broken Arrow had chosen this particular route. Then he heard the thunder and lightning ahead of them. The storm was still raging.

Maybe that was why Broken Arrow had led him this way, Hawke thought. Tunnels were a lot safer than riding around in the open when lethal shafts were hitting the ground at regular intervals.

Hawke looked around them at the rocks. The

tunnel seemed to have been carved out of the canyon wall by the hands of men, yet no man had ever touched its walls. Only countless years of slow erosion had created the natural tunnel in which the two horsemen now found themselves.

They both looked ahead. They could catch glimpses of the flashing lightning beyond the end of the tunnel.

Broken Arrow swung down from his mount and dragged a water bag from its shoulders. He then poured a few pints of its precious liquid on to the solid ground and watched as the stallion quenched its thirst.

Hawke was slower to dismount.

Unlike his companion he was tired and every sinew in his body ached. He dropped his hat on to the stone floor of the tunnel and filled its bowl with water from the bag Broken Arrow had given him during the hours of merciless sunlight.

The horses drank and their masters watched.

Hawke leaned against his saddle and sighed heavily as a dozen scattered thoughts raced through his tired mind. The drifter lifted the bag up on to his horse's neck and glanced at the silent Indian.

'You want to know something, Broken Arrow?'

Hawke mused.

The Indian did not speak. He just stood like a statue shrouded in the darkness.

'I had a real good life back home,' Hawke recalled. 'Me and my older brother had us the best of times. Then one day he up and rode off on one of Pa's best horses.'

Broken Arrow draped his water bag over his horse's shoulders. He was listening, but his gaze remained fixed upon the ground as the black stallion licked the last droplets of water off the rocky surface.

'My brother was the best pal anyone ever had.' Hawke sighed. 'I thought he might come home, but after years of waiting I decided to ride out to find him. I must have ridden halfway across the country and I ain't come close to finding him.'

The whites of Broken Arrow's eyes flashed at the youngster. He held the mane of his horse and waited for his riding partner to finish talking.

'My brother was called Luke. Reckon he must be dead. Why else would he never come home?' Hawke reached down and picked his Stetson up off the ground. He placed it on his head and gave a mock laugh. 'That must be it, he must be dead.'

There was a silence only broken by the sound of distant thunder coming through the tunnel opening ahead. Broken Arrow pulled his bow from his shoulder and lifted an arrow from the beaded quiver on his belt. He placed the arrow on the taut string of the bow and waved an arm at Hawke.

The drifter saw the signal and gave and touched the brim of his hat in reply. As he turned to face his horse he wondered why Broken Arrow had armed himself.

Did he sense danger?

Broken Arrow held his horse's mane firmly and swung up on to its back. He gathered his crude reins in his hand and tapped his moccasins against the sides of his mount. The stallion loyally started to walk on towards the light.

'I got me a feeling our confabs are a bit one-sided, Broken Arrow,' Hawke observed. He grabbed his saddle horn, raised his boot and pulled himself up on top of his mount. He stared at the back of the strange figure before him.

'I sure wish you could speak, Broken Arrow,' he muttered as he gently spurred his horse forward. 'I'd really like to know why you're covered in all that black paint. I'd also like to know why you saved my bacon by giving me this water bag back there on the prairie. Yep, if you could only speak I'd learn a lot and no mistake.'

The roof of the tunnel became lower as the two horsemen steered their mounts towards the light. Hawke watched as Broken Arrow ducked.

Once again Hawke was following.

Both horsemen were again riding towards the bright light ahead. With each step their horses took they could hear the sound of the storm growing more intense.

Hawke wondered where Broken Arrow was leading him. To safety or to some unimaginable nightmare he was incapable of understanding?

Either way Erle Hawke would follow.

For some unknown reason he trusted the silent rider more than he had ever trusted anyone before. The only time he had previously felt he could trust his life to anyone had been long ago, back on his parents' farm. The last person he had truly trusted was his brother.

He spurred and trailed the black stallion.

SIXTEEN

The brutal storm, which had tormented the prairie, was subsiding but it was not finished yet. The black clouds were finally moving away from the mission of San Angelo to continue their violent journey across the sky. As the thunder and lightning grew less frequent in the night sky none of the five outlaws knew that soon there would be a far more dangerous threat for them to endure.

Unseen by the outlaws the ghostly tribe reached the canyon floor, dismounted and started to move slowly towards their unsuspecting quarry at the mission.

The campfire raged around the blackened skillet as

Dooley dished up the ham and beans to his hungry underlings. The smell of pork fat frying gave a false sense of security to the ruthless killers as they devoured their supper like ravenous wolves.

But as they consumed their meal all them were unaware that nothing in the prairie around San Angelo was as it seemed to be. The lull in the storm was only just the start of what was about to occur.

Soon Dooley and his followers would discover for themselves that it did not pay to kill.

Revenge was stalking the outlaws as, in all ignorance, they ate their meal. It was approaching in the guise of eleven aged warriors who moved like ghosts through the brush towards the ruins of the mission.

Each of the figures was a shadow of what he had once been but the flint arrowheads perched in each of their hunting bows were just as sharp as they had ever been.

This time only the prey was different. They were no longer hunting game for food, but hunting the deadly men who had mindlessly slain two of their remaining numbers.

The Indians fanned out as they silently closed the distance between the outlaws and themselves. They moved like panthers through the darkness towards the place where they knew their prey were gathered. Scarlet sparks rose into the night air from the campfire, luring the Indians towards it like moths to a flame.

Each of the skilled hunters knelt in the darkness and readied his bow with the deadly arrows. They knelt just beyond the light of the fire's light and took aim.

The light from the rising flames danced in their hooded eyes as they watched the unsuspecting quintet lick the grease off their tin plates.

Dooley and his rancid gang of would-be graverobbers were totally unaware of the danger that loomed over them. All they could think of was the undiscovered treasure Dooley had assured them was buried somewhere close to the bell tower. They had no clue that the pendulum of fate was about to swing back in their direction.

They were about to pay for all of the outrages they had left in their bloody wake.

Dooley rose to his feet and chewed on the remainders of his meal. He wiped his sleeve across his mouth and pulled a cigar from his pocket. He poked the cigar between his teeth and walked to where his four followers sat. He struck a match and sucked in its flame. The smoke of his cigar felt good as it drifted through his teeth.

Dooley looked around the ruins. Somewhere beneath the windswept prairie he was convinced a treasure was waiting for his greedy hands to uncover it.

He glanced at the four men seated with their backs to the adobe wall.

'We start digging at sunup,' Dooley growled.

There was no objection. Although no one had spoken of it, every one of the outlaws wanted nothing more than to ride out of this cheerless place as soon as possible.

They nodded to Dooley.

The outlaw leader smiled with the cigar gripped firmly in his teeth. He was about to speak again when something drew his attention.

Suddenly the air was filled with a strange buzzing noise.

'What the hell is that?' Dooley asked. He swung on his boot heels to face towards the unearthly sound. His question would soon be answered.

Like a swarm of crazed hornets a volley of arrows flew through the air, glowing scarlet in the light of the campfire, homing in on the group of outlaws and horses.

There was no time to shout warnings.

There was even less time to move. The only thing any of them could do was watch in paralysed awe as the arrows arced unerringly towards them.

Horrific sounds of distress came from the horses. A muffled groan rose from one of Dooley's men.

The cigar fell from Dooley's lips. It had not reached the ground before the sound of arrows thudding into flesh filled the night air.

For the first time in his cruel existence Dooley was afraid. Terror rippled through him as he realized what was happening.

Stunned and helpless he watched as blood sprayed into the firelight, his eyes darting at his men and horses.

The sound of death filled the area as a deafening clap of thunder shook the ruins of the mission. Lightning spread like wildfire across the sky.

For a brief second Dooley could see clearly.

The sight skewered his guts with horror.

His eyes widened in disbelief. Two of the horses were wounded and bleeding from the arrows that had driven into their flesh. The animals' sickening moans rippled through the startled outlaws. Then

Dooley saw the body of Poke Janson stretched out on the ground with three arrows embedded in his chest.

'Injuns!' Dooley screamed. He drew one of his guns and cocked its hammer. He raised the weapon and fired blindly into the brush. He did not stop squeezing his trigger until the gun was empty. His shaking fingers fumbled as he started to reload. 'Wherever them Injuns are we gotta kill the critters before they kill the lot of us.'

Lee Chandler plucked an arrow from his leg. A fountain of blood issued from the savage wound. He managed to rise to his feet as Dooley reached his side.

'I'm hit, Sheb,' Chandler said fearfully. 'I'm bleeding like a stuck pig.'

There was no hint of concern from Dooley. He snapped his gun shut, aimed at the foes they could not see and feverishly fired again.

'Poke's dead!' Dooley exclaimed as Reece and Landon raced towards them. Dooley glanced at them. 'Are you boys hit?'

'We're OK,' Reece answered. He drew his guns from their holsters.

'I'm wounded,' Chandler yelled again.

'Then tend to it,' Dooley ordered as he fanned his gun hammer and took aim at the unseen Indians.

Landon spat with fury. He snatched a rifle from one of the saddles and cradled it in his arms. The outlaw cranked the rifle's mechanism.

'Where the hell are they, Sheb?' the outlaw asked. He raised the gun to his shoulder and fired into the darkness.

'Damned if I know, Joe,' Dooley snarled. 'All I know is that we gotta find cover before they open up again and pick more of us off.'

Suddenly the chilling sound of arrows cutting through the air filled the outlaws' ears again. The terrified men threw themselves on to the ground. More arrows hit the adobe wall behind them.

Dooley wiped the grit from his mouth. 'That was close.'

'Too damn close,' Landon added, and cocked his rifle again.

'Where did them arrows come from?' Reece growled. His eyes vainly searched the distance ahead of them. 'Where are they?'

Each of the outlaws looked around the prairie in search of their attackers. They could not see anything beyond the flickering flames of the campfire.

They had no idea that the braves were moving on, having unleashed their arrows.

'Good question, Eb. Where are them Injuns?' Dooley snarled. He rose to his feet.

Chandler tied his bandanna around his thigh and struggled to stand up in his boots.

'I reckon it must be the same bunch of critters you shot at, Sheb.' He groaned in agony. 'They want blood. Our blood.'

Dooley gritted his teeth. 'They don't just want our blood, Lee. They want our scalps.'

Landon looked at their horses.

'Two of our nags have been hit. They're dying.' He fired his rifle again. 'We'll have to ride out of here and find cover.'

Dooley glared at Landon venomously. 'Run away? You want to run away? I ain't letting a bunch of stinking Injuns run me off. We're here to collect the treasure, boys. I intend staying here until we find that damn treasure.'

Reece moved closer to Dooley.

'Joe's right, Sheb. How are we gonna ride out of here with the gold if we ain't got any horses left?' he reasoned as he allowed Chandler to rest an arm on his shoulder. 'Them varmints will kill every damn nag we got. Without horses we're as good as dead in this prairie.'

'We already lost two of our mounts,' Landon pointerd out again.

Chandler nodded. 'He's right. We have to get away from here before they do kill all of our horses, Sheb. Once the sun rises we can turn the tables on them damn Injuns.'

Dooley returned his nod. 'You're right.'

'We can come back after sunup,' Landon said. His finger curled around the trigger of his Winchester as he searched vainly for a target. 'Them varmints won't stand a chance when we can see 'em.'

Reluctantly Dooley agreed.

'OK. Saddle the damn horses,' he said. 'Let's get out of here.'

SEVENTEEN

The clatter of horses' hoofs echoed as both riders drew close to the end of the tunnel. Broken Arrow emerged from the tunnel first. He stopped his powerful stallion as the young drifter rode to his side. Both horsemen held their mounts in check as they reached the rim of the canyon. From their vantage point they could see the rocks graduate down towards the canyon floor. Hawke glanced heavenward. Now the stars could be seen again as the storm ebbed.

They had travelled a considerable distance through the underground trail to reach this spot. Still the drifter did not know why Broken Arrow had led him this way. As ever, the mysterious Indian did not utter a sound as his eyes scanned the terrain below them.

Hawke studied the profile of the man astride the big black stallion. The mask of pigment defied even the keenest of eyes to penetrate it.

Then suddenly both riders were startled as they heard the distinctive sound of shooting away in the distance. Broken Arrow gripped his reins firmly and urged his mount forward to the very edge of the deadly drop. Gravel fell over the rim as the stallion obeyed its master.

Hawke rose in his stirrups and stared down through the eerie starlight. The distant shots could be seen carving a route through the darkness.

'Who in tarnation is shooting?' Hawke asked, keeping his own horse well away from the rim of the canyon. 'And who are they shooting at?'

The words had only just left his lips when another volley of gunfire echoed around them.

Not a muscle moved in Broken Arrow's face. He walked his stallion back from where they had been standing.

Like an eagle seeking out its next meal, Broken Arrow focused his gaze. Whatever he was thinking, it remained a secret from his companion.

More shots rang out.

Hawke moved his mount closer to the Indian.

'Where's that shooting coming from?' the young drifter wondered aloud.

Broken Arrow pointed with his bow at the exact place where, with his keen eyesight, he could see the red tapers of bullets as they tore through the distant gloom.

Hawke looked at the dark face. He suddenly realized that his companion could understand what he was saying.

'You *do* savvy my lingo, Broken Arrow,' Hawke said. 'I sure was starting to wonder about that.'

The Indian gave a nod of his head and jabbed again at the air with his bow. Hawke stood in his stirrups and peered out into the depths of the canyon. Broken Arrow was aiming his bow at the bell tower.

Hawke saw it at last.

'I see it. What the hell is that?' he asked. 'Is that a building?'

Broken Arrow nodded and turned his horse. He was about to ride when he saw the two unshod Indian ponies standing near by.

Hawke watched as the expression on Broken Arrow's face changed dramatically. Not even the mask of paint could hide the concern in his features. Without warning the rider of the black stallion hit the tail of his mount with his bow and rode across the rocks towards the ponies.

'Where are you going?' Hawke called out as he followed. Then he too saw the ponies.

To Hawke's surprise Broken Arrow jumped from his stallion's back and ran to something close to where the two ponies stood.

Hawke watched as Broken Arrow knelt. Puzzled, the drifter steered his horse close to the black stallion.

'What is it?' Hawke yelled. 'What's got you so all fired up, Broken Arrow?'

His question seemed answered when he saw the two bodies wrapped in blankets on the rim of the rocks. Hawke drew rein and dismounted. The starlight danced across the spilled blood which lay everywhere. Hawke swallowed hard as his eyes focused upon the grim vision. He led his horse to where Broken Arrow knelt, and stared at the two dead Indians.

Hawke had not seen many corpses before. This was the first time he had ever seen any with bullet holes in their lifeless forms.

A cold shiver traced along his spine. It had nothing to do with the temperature.

His gloved hand gripped his reins tightly. The starlight was enough for the drifter to clearly see the two bullet holes in the Indians' chests. Hawke rubbed his neck and looked again to where the gunfire was still raging.

'This has something to do with the five riders I was trailing,' he reasoned. 'That's why you tried to stop me. You figured that I'd end up like these two poor Injuns.'

Broken Arrow placed the blankets back over the faces of the dead men and rose to his feet. He stared out at the red tapers that were still tracing through the darkness near the mission. The sound of the guns being fired crackled in his ears.

Hawke shook his head. 'You saved my bacon twice, friend. I had no idea you were looking out for my hide.'

The figure turned and stared straight at Hawke.

'That's right, Erle,' Broken Arrow said unexpectedly. Then he moved towards his horse.

Hawke gasped in surprise that his companion could actually talk. He stepped closer to the tall Indian and grabbed his naked arm. Then another thought occurred to him.

'How'd you know my name?' he wondered. 'I ain't told you my name.'

Broken Arrow turned. He stared at Hawke from behind his mask of black paint.

'Who else would ride into a prairie without water or grub?' he asked quietly.

No bolt of lightning could have shocked the drifter so much as the sound of the familiar voice. The young drifter realized who he was looking at. Suddenly the black pigment no longer prevented his eyes from seeing the truth.

'Luke?' he gasped.

Broken Arrow nodded. 'I wondered how long it would take you to figure out who I was, little brother.'

Hawke covered his mouth with his gloved hand. He was shaking.

'I don't understand,' he admitted. 'Why are you dressed like that?'

'It's a long story,' Broken Arrow said. 'Too long for me to explain right now.'

Hawke watched as Broken Arrow grabbed the mane of his powerful stallion and threw himself up on to its back.

'But I—'

'There's no time.' Broken Arrow turned the stallion and pointed down at the mission. 'I have to try and save the lives of those who are left of this tribe.'

'You have to?' Hawke looked puzzled. 'Why?'

'They once saved my life, little brother,' Broken Arrow replied gathering his crude reins together. 'I owe them.'

Hawke watched as Broken Arrow whipped the tail of his stallion and raced down the rocks towards the canyon floor. He mounted his own horse, swung around and spurred.

EIGHTEEN

The stench of gunsmoke hung in the night air around the mission. The four outlaws had fired more than fifty bullets into the darkness in an attempt to kill their attackers, yet there was no sign that they had achieved their goal. The notorious outlaws reloaded their weaponry as Landon led the remaining horses towards them.

Dooley rose from behind the adobe wall and waved his men to the horses. He watched the sagebrush for any sign of the Indians as his men mounted the animals.

When they were atop their saddles the ruthless killer ran and jumped up behind Reece. He patted his top gun on the shoulder.

'Let's ride,' he called out.

The outlaws responded immediately.

For more than five minutes there had been no response to the outlaws' barrage of lethal lead. Then, as soon as the horses responded to their masters' spurs, the deadly arrows came hurtling from out of the surrounding shadows.

Before any of the riders knew what was happening, each of their horses was hit by the arrows. They gave out hideous and painful sounds as they staggered and fell to the ground.

Dooley and Reece were thrown over the neck of their horse as Landon and Chandler felt their own mount crumpled beneath them.

They hit the ground hard. Dooley rolled over the shoulder of Reece, Chandler's mount narrowly missing him as it fell lifelessly beside him.

Landon was first to crawl away from his injured gelding. Blood was pouring freely from the stricken animal as it kicked out from the pain that racked its body.

'I thought they were dead,' Landon called out to the other outlaws.

Dooley shook his head. Blood was pouring from a gash across his chest where an arrow had ripped

144

through his jacket.

He was dazed. He struggled to his knees and stared down at the wound.

'What happened?' Dooley groaned as Landon scrambled to his side.

Landon had lost his rifle but he still had his faithful .45 gripped firmly in his hand.

'Are you OK, Sheb?' Landon asked his groggy leader.

Dooley was about to reply when he saw the body of Reece spread out beside them. He lifted the arm of his top gun and watched it fall limply when he released his grip.

'They killed Eb,' Dooley raged.

Landon dragged Reece over on to his back. The feathered flight of an arrow protruded from the blood-soaked chest.

'They surely did.'

It was as if the arrow that had ended Reece's life had ignited a fuse inside Dooley. He rose to his feet and drew both his guns.

'Them Injuns are gonna pay for that,' Dooley shouted.

Landon saw the glint of an arrowhead as a bow was raised just beyond the campfire. He wrestled

Dooley off his feet as the high-pitched whirr of an arrow filled his ears.

The arrow hit the adobe wall so hard that it became embedded in the ancient bricks.

Dooley stared up at the arrow and then into Landon's face as he realized how close he had come to joining Reece.

'Get me out of here, Joe,' Dooley ordered.

'Where can we go?' Landon asked. Then he fired in the direction of the archer.

Dooley pointed one of his guns at the bell tower. 'Let's take cover in there.'

Both outlaws desperately crawled on their bellies towards the tower. They did not stop until they had entered the tall building.

Lee Chandler heaved his legs from beneath his fallen mount and gazed all around the mission. The small patch of ground was soaked with the blood of horses and men alike.

Chandler swallowed hard.

'Where are you, Sheb?' he called out.

'We're in the tower,' Dooley responded. He had propped himself up against the interior of the tall tower. 'Get over here before you end up like Eb.'

Chandler moved to the belly of his mount and

tried vainly to see where the Indians were. He got up on to his knees and looked over the saddle.

He drew his gun, fanned its hammer and fired three times into the brush. If he had hit any of the Indians they had not made any noise, he thought. His gaze darted to the bell tower. It was barely twenty feet from where he knelt.

Chandler glanced at his blood-soaked pants leg and the savage wound, which had torn into his thigh. The fall from his horse had not done it any favours, he thought. It was bleeding even more now than it had been after he had dragged the arrow from his flesh.

He rose up to a crouching position and started to run as best he could towards the bell tower. As he sped he turned and squeezed the trigger of his gun. As a deafening flash erupted from its barrel he felt the powerful arrows as they found his guts.

Dooley and Landon looked on in horror as they saw the arrows send him crashing into the wall. Chandler slid down the adobe bricks to the ground.

Landon looked out from the cover of the tower.

'He ain't dead, Sheb.'

On seeing the lethal arrows poking out of his guts, Chandler raised his smoking gun to his head.

147

The sound of the shot rang out and Chandler fell on to his face. His lifeless arm dropped the smoking gun into the pool of blood that surrounded him.

'He's dead now, Joe,' Dooley said and spat.

Joe Landon cocked both his guns and looked out at the brush. 'I'm gonna kill them critters. I'm gonna kill them coz they've killed us.'

In quick succession Landon emptied both his guns' bullets at their unseen enemies. Once again there was no reply. The younger outlaw turned to Dooley as he shook the spent casings from his hot chambers and pulled fresh bullets from his belt.

Dooley gritted his teeth.

'We've fired so many bullets into that brush they just have to be dead, Joe,' Dooley insisted. 'We must have killed them all by now.'

Landon looked at Dooley.

'Listen,' he said. 'Do you hear that?'

Dooley lowered his head. He could also hear the echoing pounding of horses' hoofs as they drew nearer.

'I hear horses, Joe.'

Landon cocked both his guns again.

'And they're heading this way, Sheb. Who do you reckon they are?'

The outlaw leader nodded knowingly as he listened to the sound of the pounding hoofs coming closer to the bell tower.

'I don't give a damn who them varmints are, Joe,' Dooley answered. He grinned as he checked both his guns and readied them for action. 'The only thing I give a hoot about is that they got horses and we need horses.'

Joe Landon moved to a window set in the tower wall. His eyes narrowed as they focused on the two riders.

'And they're riding this way.'

'Let 'em come, Joe.' Dooley cocked his gun hammers. 'Let 'em come.'

FINALE

Broken Arrow had never ridden as quickly as he did now. He charged through the starlight as the last remnants of the lightning storm flickered in the heavens above. The high bell tower was momentarily illuminated by one brilliant flash. Every inch of the canyon was bathed in the blinding light of tremendous power. The black stallion thundered towards it.

At that same moment Hawke saw the unmistakable sight of two gun barrels poking out from the tower window. They were trained on Broken Arrow.

'Luke,' he yelled. 'Look out!'

The warning came a fraction of a second before the guns fired. Two venomous plumes of white death spewed from the weapons' barrels and cut through the starlight.

Broken Arrow heard the shots and ducked. Both of Joe Landon's bullets had been aimed high for fear of hitting the stallion.

As the bullets passed over his war bonnet Broken Arrow leapt from his mount and rolled across the ground. With a fluid action the dark figure pulled an arrow from his quiver and sent it buzzing towards the outlaws. The arrow took the Stetson off the outlaw's head. Hawke drew level with his brother just as two more shots came from the small window.

Broken Arrow leapt towards Hawke.

Hawke felt himself being dragged from his mount as the bullets passed just above his saddle. Broken Arrow flung the drifter to the ground and threw himself at his brother's horse. He grabbed at its bridle.

His powerful arms stopped the mount in its tracks.

Broken Arrow ripped the saddle rope from the saddle horn and tossed it at Hawke. He then stepped in the stirrup and whipped the mount's tail with his bow.

Hawke pulled himself up with the coiled rope in his hands. He watched in awe as Broken Arrow balanced in the stirrup and crouched as the horse galloped towards the bell tower.

Broken Arrow was using the stallion as a shield.

The horse raced across the sand towards the mission. Just before it reached the tower Broken Arrow dropped to the ground and ran up to the ruined wall.

He watched as the skittish stallion continued to run away from the gun play. His mind raced. It was obvious that someone was in the bell tower but Broken Arrow wondered how many were actually inside it.

Broken Arrow ran to one of the ruined walls and leapt like a puma over it. As his moccasins landed on the opposite side of the wall Broken Arrow pulled an arrow from his quiver.

He placed it on the bow's taut string and drew the string back. For more than a minute he simply waited, with his ancient weapon ready.

Then he saw Landon as the outlaw moved back to the window with his smoking .45s still in his hands. Broken Arrow was about to release the deadly projectile when Landon vanished from view behind one of the tower's walls.

Broken Arrow began to approach the bell tower.

With each step his narrowed eyes darted around every aspect of the adobe ruins. Broken Arrow was like a rattlesnake as his feet slid silently across the soft earth.

He was ready to strike at his target when he should have a clear shot. Steadily he continued to approach the base of the tower.

Suddenly Joe Landon appeared again and swiftly turned to face Broken Arrow. Both men stared at one another. Landon gasped at the horrific sight of the bowman. Without any hesitation Landon cocked his guns and raised them.

Broken Arrow released the bowstring. The bow shook in his hand as the arrow took flight.

Within seconds Broken Arrow had plucked another arrow from his quiver and charged his weapon again. He drew back on the string as his first arrow hit Landon squarely in the chest. As Landon stumbled backwards both his guns blasted into the ground. With unblinking eyes Broken Arrow watched as the outlaw hit the tower wall and slid all the way down it. The starlight reflected off the bloodstained bricks.

Unseen by the archer, Dooley watched as Landon slumped into his own gore. With his guns in his hands the outlaw leader pressed his back against the adobe wall and waited.

Broken Arrow was about to approach when he caught a brief glimpse of two more gun barrels poking round the doorframe. He fired his arrow directly at the guns and then dived over the wall. As he hit the ground two bullets blew chunks out of the adobe brickwork above his war bonnet.

He drew another arrow from his quiver and placed it on the taut string of his bow. He rose, fired at the tower and returned to his knees.

Hawke ran to his brother's side, still holding the cutting rope. He leaned over the crouching archer.

'How many are there?' Hawke panted.

Broken Arrow did not answer. Instead he grabbed the rope and uncoiled it. He crawled into the shadows, stood and looked to the top of the tall tower and began to swing the rope with all the skill of a wrangler.

As the cutting rope gathered momentum Broken Arrow looked at his young brother. He smiled, then released the large looped end of his lariat. The rope flew up and encircled one of the broken bricks.

Broken Arrow pulled the noose tight and placed the bow over his arm. Hawke watched as Broken Arrow swiftly climbed up the side of the tower.

Suddenly bullets hit the adobe bricks of the wall beside Hawke. The drifter crouched as debris showered over him. He took to his heels and ran twenty feet to the end of the ruin. He knelt and leaned around its corner.

Hawke fired his gun.

He saw Dooley duck back into the bell tower.

Hawke had Dooley pinned down. He cocked his gun again and fired. His bullet ricocheted off the base of the tower. As the gunsmoke filtered from the barrel of his gun he saw his brother reach the top of the tower and clamber on to it.

Far above the main mission building Broken Arrow stood on what was left of the wooden floor of the bell chamber. He looked down through the gap where once a staircase had existed. It was now a void, dark apart from the starlit base far below him.

Broken Arrow could see the deadly outlaw leaning against the wall thirty feet below him. Dooley was holding his guns in his hands.

The last of the outlaws was getting ready to fire again. He was preparing to kill. Broken Arrow pulled the rope up from the outside of the bell tower. A grim thought festered in his mind.

What if he was looking down upon the outlaw who had shot the two Indians he had found? Whoever had shot them had been a marksman of incredible skill.

Broken Arrow glanced down at his brother near the ruined wall. The youngster had provided him with cover as he had kept the outlaw trapped inside the tower.

Again he considered the man standing far below his perilous perch.

If the outlaw was the man who had shot the Indians with such ease, his brother did not stand a chance. Dooley was deadly.

Broken Arrow wrapped the rope around his waist and checked that the jagged loop was still holding firm. He gave the rope a firm tug, then lowered his head.

Then he jumped into the abyss.

At tremendous speed Broken Arrow plummeted through the darkness. As he fell his eyes continued to look down at Dooley. There was no fear in the man covered in black pigment. All he knew was that he had to stop the outlaw from firing his guns again.

Within a few heartbeats Broken Arrow had reached his target. Both his feet caught the startled Dooley on his shoulders. The interior of the tower resounded to the sound of breaking bones. The force knocked the outlaw off his feet and sent him crashing into the ground.

Broken Arrow was swinging back and forth at the end of the rope a few feet above Dooley. He released the knot and dropped to the ground, to land close by where Dooley lay.

He had imagined that anyone being struck with such force would be killed instantly. Broken Arrow had been wrong.

Suddenly, to his total surprise, he saw Dooley raise both his guns and aim them at him.

Faster than the blink of an eye Broken Arrow pulled his bow off his shoulder and placed an arrow upon its string. Then the sound of a shot rang out.

Sheb Dooley fell at Broken Arrow's feet. A neat bullet hole smouldered in the centre of the outlaw's lifeless back as life drifted away on the smoke.

Broken Arrow looked as Hawke walked nervously through the gunsmoke of his weapon.

'Did I get him, Luke?' Hawke asked.

'You did, little brother.'

Hawke followed his brother out into the sand and watched as he strode beyond the campfire. The young drifter waited for what seemed a lifetime, then he saw the blackened figure walk slowly back towards him.

He moved quickly to Broken Arrow's side.

'What's wrong, Luke?' he asked.

Broken Arrow exhaled and shook his head.

'They're all dead.' He sighed. 'I buried them out there.'

'You mean the Injuns?' Hawke ran his fingers through his sweat-soaked hair. 'They're all dead?'

'Yep.' Broken Arrow paced across the blood-stained sand towards his black stallion. He took hold of its mane, then paused. 'I told you that they saved my life.'

'How did they do that?' Hawke asked.

Broken Arrow forced a smile. 'A long time ago another young drifter was trying to cross that prairie. Just like you he didn't have any water or grub. They saved my bacon. They taught me how to survive out here.'

Hawke looked at his brother. A brother who was almost unrecognizable from the memories he still held dear in his soul.

'Is that why you become an Injun?' Hawke wondered. 'To be like them?'

Broken Arrow ruffled his brother's hair. He smiled.

'Maybe it is, Erle,' he said. He swung up on to the back of his black stallion. 'I learned a lot from them. I tried to be like them. Now they're all gone.'

'They say nothing really dies if someone remembers them, Luke.' Hawke shrugged. 'You remember them and that's what matters.'

Then out in the darkness they heard the sound of horses' hoofs as they came down the canyon towards the mission. Hawke was nervous as he moved closer to the black stallion and its master.

'Who is that?' he gulped. 'I hope it ain't more outlaws.'

Broken Arrow narrowed his eyes and squinted down the canyon at the three approaching horsemen. He glanced down at his brother.

'Don't fret. I can see their tin stars from here,' Broken Arrow said. 'We'll let them clean up this mess.'

Hawke sighed as Broken Arrow reached down.

'Does my wise little brother want to ride double until we find that damn horse of yours?' he asked.

'Thank you kindly, brother Luke,' Hawke replied as he was pulled him up on to the horse. 'Any idea where we're headed?'

Broken Arrow tapped his heels against the sides of his mount.

'Reckon it's about time I took you home.'